DECEPTION

Falon,

Things are never what
they seem...

NEW YORK TIMES AND USA TODAY BESTSELLING AUTHOR

K.A. ROBINSON

Cover Designer: Romantic Book Affairs – Letitia Hasser

Editor and Interior Designer: Jovana Shirley, Unforeseen Editing, www.unforeseenediting.com

Visit my website at: www.authorkarobinson.blogspot.com or www.facebook.com/karobinson13

ISBN-13: 978-1502315267

OTHER BOOKS BY

NEW YORK TIMES AND *USA TODAY* BESTSELLING AUTHOR
K.A. ROBINSON

THE TORN SERIES

TORN
TWISTED
TAINTED
TOXIC
TAMED
COMING NOVEMBER 2014

THE TIES SERIES

SHATTERED TIES
TWISTED TIES

BREAKING ALEXANDRIA

Taming Alec

CONTENTS

Chapter One 1

Chapter Two.. 15

Chapter Three 33

Chapter Four 43

Chapter Five 57

Chapter Six 67

Chapter Seven 81

Chapter Eight 91

Chapter Nine 101

Chapter Ten.. 113

Chapter Eleven 123

Chapter Twelve 137

Chapter Thirteen.. 151

Chapter Fourteen... 161

Chapter Fifteen 171

Chapter Sixteen 183

Chapter Seventeen.. 199

Chapter Eighteen... 209

Chapter Nineteen... 219

Chapter Twenty 235

Chapter Twenty-One 251

Tamed Teaser... 263

Acknowledgments 275

A note to readers:

Before you start reading *Deception*, I want to make you aware of something. Claire can be a bit ignorant at times. As a young woman who has never really had a role model to help her learn and grow into an adult, she can be very naive. She also has a habit of making choices that will definitely make her seem weak and, at times, annoying. Please remember that as a series moves forward, the characters often grow and evolve. Claire is most certainly one of those characters.

With that being said, I hope you learn to love Claire as I have. She is one of the most diverse characters I've ever written, and I can't wait to show you what I have in store for her.

Lots of hugs,

K.A.

My feet were killing me. All I wanted to do was go home, take a shower, and crawl into bed.

Work had been brutal tonight. I'd been working at the same diner for almost two years, but up until last week, I'd only been part-time. The day after I'd graduated from Morgantown High School, I'd switched to full-time.

I didn't really mind waitressing, but my body was still getting used to being on the move constantly. The diner, a small family-owned business, was always busy with the same customers. Most of them knew me by now and usually tipped well. A few college kids would come in from time to time, but they usually went to one of the more popular spots in Morgantown. I didn't mind though because they were normally the ones who would leave crappy tips.

I pulled into the driveway of my foster parents' house and yawned. I hoped they were asleep. My foster dad, Rick, was an asshole to me most of the time. The only reason he kept me and the other foster kids around was because of the nice checks he would receive for taking care of us. I knew my time here would be up soon. Today was my eighteenth birthday. Hopefully, my foster dad hadn't remembered. I didn't feel like getting kicked out of the only place I had to go tonight.

My foster mom, Tammy, wasn't as bad as Rick. She could even be nice at times, but her fear of Rick's temper would keep her from defending any of the kids. Rick wasn't physically abusive, but when his temper got the best of him, he'd go on a rampage that rivaled a three-year-old's. Tammy had learned long ago to lock up anything breakable.

I'd been in twelve different foster homes since I was three. Tammy and Rick's house wasn't the best, but it definitely wasn't the worst. I shuddered as I thought about my last two houses. Yeah, I could deal with Rick's asshole ways. I didn't give a gigglefuck about Rick's temper as long as he wouldn't try to touch me.

I climbed out of my piece-of-shit car and headed for the house. My car was the only thing I truly owned. I'd saved every penny I could and purchased it two months ago. I'd paid six hundred dollars for a 1989 Chevy Impala, and I definitely got what I'd paid for. The body was rusted out in several places. The right rear fender was an ugly green color while the rest of the car was a faded red. It was the ugliest Christmas-themed car I'd ever seen. Actually, it was the ugliest car I'd ever seen—period. But it would get me from point A to point B most of the time. Sadly, it wasn't even street legal, but I didn't have the extra cash to get everything I needed to make it so.

Once I reached the house, I stuck my key into the lock and turned it. I frowned when the door didn't unlock. I pulled the key out, thinking that maybe I'd shoved it in the wrong way, and I tried again. Realization hit me when the lock still didn't turn over. Rick had changed it while I was at work.

I sighed in defeat before knocking loudly on the door. Lights turned on in the living room, and then I heard the door unlocking.

Rick opened the door and frowned at me. "Yes?"

"Um…the door wouldn't open for me," I said.

"Probably not since I changed the lock."

"Why would you do that?" I asked even though I knew the answer.

"You're eighteen now, Claire. You're no longer my problem."

I laughed humorlessly. "Seriously? You're kicking me out on my birthday?"

"Yeah, I guess I am," he said without remorse.

"Can I at least get my clothes and stuff?"

He shrugged. "Make it quick."

He moved out of the way, and I hurried past him toward the room that I shared with Shelly.

Shelly was a foster kid, too. She'd been here when I arrived. She was only ten, but I'd found myself gravitating toward her from the beginning. We would look out for each other. I hated to think about her being here alone. I was pretty sure I was the only person in this house who cared about her.

I passed by the boys' bedroom on the way to my room. Besides Shelly and me, two other foster kids lived here. Kevin was thirteen, and Jerimiah was eight. I wasn't as close to them as I was to Shelly, but I'd still miss them as well.

I opened the door to my room and flipped on the light switch. Shelly was sound asleep in the bottom bunk. I moved quietly around the room, shoving my clothes and personal items into the suitcase I'd carried around since I was first put into foster care. It didn't take me long to pack. I had very few clothes and even less personal items.

My eyes misted as I picked up the only thing I had left of my mom—a locket. I opened it up to see the tiny photo of her and me. I was only a few months old in the picture. My mom had been killed in a car accident right before I turned three. Her parents were also dead, and no one knew who my father was. With no family to take me in, I had been thrown into the foster system.

I closed my eyes and tried to remember my mother. As always, nothing came to me, except for the way she'd smelled. All I knew about her was that she'd smelled like strawberries. I closed the locket and slipped it into my jeans pocket. Once it was safely tucked away, I closed my suitcase and glanced down at Shelly. I hated to wake her up, but I couldn't leave without saying good-bye.

I crouched down next to her and gently poked her a few times.

Her eyes slowly opened, and she stared up at me. "Claire? What's wrong?" she asked as she sat up.

"I have to leave, kiddo. My time's up," I said as I tried to smile at her.

"What? Why?" she asked, panic filling her voice.

"Rick's giving me the boot. I gotta go."

"He can't do that!" she cried angrily.

"I'm eighteen, so technically, he can."

Shelly's eyes filled with tears as she sprang off the bed and wrapped her tiny arms around me. "I'm going to miss you so much."

I hugged her back tightly. "I'll miss you, too. Take care of yourself, and keep out of trouble, okay?"

"You know I will. Will I see you again?"

I pulled away and cupped her cheek. "I don't know. Maybe someday."

She nodded as her shoulders sagged in defeat. "Please be careful."

"Always. I love you."

"Love you, too," she whispered.

I pushed her back into bed and tucked her in. I kissed her forehead before pulling away. I stood and grabbed my suitcase off the floor. I gave her one last smile before I opened the door and slipped silently into the hallway.

Rick was still standing by the front door when I walked into the living room.

"Did you get everything?" he asked.

"Yeah."

"Good, because you're not welcome back here. Got me?"

"Yeah, I got you." I shoved past him.

I didn't look back as I walked to my car. I tossed my suitcase into the backseat before climbing behind the wheel. I backed out of the driveway and headed toward the main part of town. I couldn't stop the tears from falling as I realized just how screwed I was.

I had fifty bucks to my name until I would get paid next week. I just hoped that I could make decent tips until then, or I'd be living on air. There was no way I'd be able to afford an apartment, even a shitty one, for at least a few months. I had no money, no friends, no credit, nothing. I was completely alone. The only thing I did have was my car.

I gently patted the dashboard. "Looks like it's just you and me now, ugly Christmas car."

I drove back to work and parked behind the building. There was no way I would park on the street. With my luck, a cop would come by and notice that every sticker on my car was expired. I didn't need a tow bill that I couldn't pay for. I shut off the engine and reclined the seat back until I was looking up at the roof of the car.

At least it's not cold out, I thought to myself as I closed my eyes.

My entire body was rigid as I tried to control the emotions raging inside me. I tried to find the positives, but aside from the fact that I wouldn't have to deal with Rick anymore, there were none. I attempted to shut off my mind, so I could sleep.

I would be working the morning shift tomorrow. I needed the money too much to oversleep and miss my shift. Plus, I wouldn't want to do that to my boss, Bob. He was a really nice guy, too nice for his own good sometimes.

I vowed to myself that I would figure things out when I woke up the next morning. I had no other choice. I had to make a plan, or I'd never survive.

Days had passed since Rick kicked me out of his house. I'd accomplished nothing unless I counted the tips I'd made. I had been living off of dollar cheeseburgers and washing myself in the restroom sink at work. A Laundromat was nearby, so I at least had clean clothes.

The first day, I'd left after my shift ended. I'd waited until the diner closed and everyone was gone before driving back and parking behind the building again. I'd made sure that I was up and gone before the diner opened the next morning since I was on night shift.

The second day had gone much the same way. Hiding at the local library all day, I'd lost myself in the pages of not one, but two books. The first one was a paranormal book about angels and demons that I'd read a million times. I would use it to escape reality. My problems would seem so small when compared to the main character's issues. So what if I was homeless? At least I didn't have to worry about stopping a hoard of demons from taking over the earth and enslaving mankind. The second book was a romance. It was about a girl my age starting fresh in college and falling in love with a man who was no good for her. I couldn't help but feel sad as I'd read it. There was no fresh start at college and no love in my future.

It was the third day, and I was working the morning shift again. I was taking my daily sink bath in the restroom when one of my coworkers, Junie, walked in on me naked.

"Oh my God!" I screamed as I tried to cover myself. Apparently, I'd forgotten to lock the restroom door.

Junie looked like she wanted to die as she quickly mumbled an apology and slammed the door shut. After I dried off with paper towels, I walked back into the main part of the diner. I headed over to the coffee pots and started making both decaf and regular, praying that Junie wouldn't mention what had happened. Naturally, she cornered me while I was dumping coffee grinds into the filter.

"Claire, why were you taking a bath in the restroom?" she asked.

I glanced up to see concern in her expression. Junie was older than me, probably in her late twenties or early thirties. With light-brown hair and brown eyes, she was pretty but plain. She'd recently gone through a nasty divorce and lost a lot of weight. I knew the stress from the divorce and trying to raise her two boys on her own had been taking a toll on her. I didn't know much about what had happened, but I was pretty sure the bastard had cheated on her.

"I didn't get a chance to shower at my house this morning," I lied.

"Cut the crap, Claire. What is going on?" she asked.

I debating on lying again, but I couldn't do it. Junie was always nice to me, and I couldn't lie right to her face again.

"Rick kicked me out of the house the other night." I looked away from her.

"He what? That asshole! I'm so sorry, Claire," Junie said.

I looked up to see her brown eyes filled with anger. "Don't apologize. There's nothing you or anyone else could've said to stop him. You and I both knew it was coming."

"You could call and report him though. I mean, he's still getting paid for this month even though you're eighteen."

"Then, what happens if the foster care people decide Tammy and Rick aren't suitable foster parents? Shelly, Kevin, and Jerimiah would be pulled out and put into a house that could be ten times worse. Rick's an ass, but he'd never hurt them. I won't be the reason they're sent to a horrible home," I said as I stared at her.

She sighed. "Fine, I see your point, but it's still not right. What are you going to do?"

I shrugged. "I have no clue. I guess I'll just keep saving my tips until I can afford a place to stay. My car will work for now since it's summer, but I'll have to find somewhere to stay before winter hits."

"I wish you could stay with me, but I literally have no room." She was clearly upset over the fact that she couldn't help me.

"Don't worry about it, Junie. I'll be fine. I need you to promise me that this won't leave the two of us. I don't want anyone to know what's going on with me. It's embarrassing."

"Claire…" She bit her lip.

"Junie, please," I begged.

"Fine, I won't say anything, but I wish I could help you somehow."

"Don't stress about it. Just focus on taking care of your kiddos. They need you more than I do."

She gave me a weak smile before walking over to a family who had just walked in. I watched as she led them to a table and handed them menus. I smiled as the mom picked her baby up out of the portable car seat and cradled the little one in her arms. A wave of sadness swept over me as I thought of all the things I'd missed out on with my own mother. I hoped that this baby would have a better life than I had.

The rest of the morning went by quickly. By the end of my shift, I was dragging. Once my last table was cleared, I walked into the back room and grabbed my purse. I headed back out to the front and waved at Sarah, the waitress taking over my tables. She waved back before turning her attention to the two guys she was waiting on.

Our boss, Bob, came barreling out of his office and headed straight for me. "Claire, I need a favor," he said when he stopped in front of me.

"Sure. What's up?" I asked.

"I hate to ask you this, but can you work the evening shift, too? Stacey just called off. I'd ask Junie, but I know she has to pick her boys up from the sitter."

My feet screamed at me to run away, but I couldn't do that to Bob. Plus, I needed the extra money.

"Of course I'll stay." I smiled at him.

"Thank you. I owe you one, Claire. Don't think that I haven't noticed how hard you've been working lately."

I nodded. "I try. I'd better go put my purse away and head back out onto the floor before Sarah gets overrun."

He nodded before turning and walking back into his office. I hurried to the back room and shoved my purse in my locker. After making a quick stop in the restroom, I walked out onto the floor. Sarah was running back and forth, trying to take care of my new tables as well as hers. I gave her an apologetic smile before heading to my side.

By the time my second shift was over, I could barely walk. It was a Friday night, and we'd been especially busy. The diner didn't serve alcohol, which kept away several potential customers, but we were constantly busy with families. Most of them would tip well, and I ended the day with almost a hundred dollars in tips. I smiled when I realized I would be eating something besides an artery-clogging hamburger when I left. I might even splurge on a salad.

"I'm beat," Sarah said as we wiped down all the tables. "I don't know how you're still standing. You've been here since we opened."

"Sheer will and determination. Plus, I made a ton of tips today."

"Nice. Go buy yourself something pretty." She high-fived me as she walked by.

I laughed and smacked her on the butt with my towel.

Once the tables were clean, the condiments and shakers filled up, and the floor mopped, I walked to the back room and grabbed my purse. After shoving my cash inside, I told everyone good night and headed out to my car.

I drove across town to Denny's and ordered the salad I'd been desperately craving. I even ordered a Coke instead of water. I was a splurging fool tonight.

I glanced up from my salad and noticed two guys watching me from a few tables over. Both of them were good-looking, and they appeared to be around my age. I guessed they were probably students at West Virginia University. Morgantown was a college town through and through, and the streets were usually crawling with kids. I assumed that these two were local since most of the students had packed up and headed home for summer vacation.

One of them noticed me staring, and he gave me a smile that sent my heart racing into overdrive. Suddenly embarrassed by my gawking, I looked away and used my blonde hair as a shield between them and me.

I'd had a few dates in high school but nothing to get excited over. I wasn't a virgin. I'd lost that to Scott Marks my junior year. One time in the backseat of his dad's Ford truck hadn't really taught me everything I needed to know—or anything I needed to know really. I definitely wasn't skilled when it came to the opposite sex.

I quickly ate my food and paid my bill without looking over at the guys' table again. My life was a disaster as it was. Adding a guy would only complicate things more.

I walked out to my car and unlocked the door before climbing inside. Once the doors were locked again, I started the engine and pulled away from the lot.

I couldn't help but grin as I remembered the guy's smile. From what I could tell, he'd been cute. His dark brown hair was shaggy, but it wasn't so long that it looked messy. His arms were toned, probably from playing football or basketball. Those were the only two sports people really cared about around here, and football was the favorite. Once football season hit, that was what everyone would talk about. I wasn't a big fan of sports, but even I cheered for the Mountaineers.

I drove back to the restaurant and parked, trying not to think about the cute guy or his smile. I yawned and reclined my seat. Yeah, there was no way in hell I could think about boys right now.

I sat up straight when I heard someone tapping on my window. Terrified that it was the cops, my heart started racing as I looked over. Relief flooded my body when I saw Junie.

I turned my key, so I could roll down the window. "Morning," I mumbled.

"Hey, I thought I'd wake you up. Our shift starts in ten minutes." She frowned down at me.

"Shit," I mumbled. I rolled my window back up and pulled my key from the ignition. I grabbed my purse off the floor and stepped out.

Junie waited as I popped my trunk and pulled out fresh underwear, a bra, and my work uniform. I had three work uniforms. After today, only one would be clean, so I made a mental note to stop at the Laundromat tonight after work.

Junie shook her head as she watched me throw my clothes into my oversized purse. I pretended not to notice her reaction as I closed my trunk. Walking toward the diner, I didn't look at her, and I headed into the restroom. After making sure that the door was locked this time, I stripped down and started washing my body off. Once that was done, I soaked my hair in the sink and scrubbed it quickly. I brushed it out and tied it up in a high bun, so no one would notice that it was wet. I brushed my teeth and then shoved my dirty clothes and toiletries back into my bag.

I glanced at myself one last time to make sure that I was presentable. I was ashamed that I'd been reduced to washing my hair and bathing in a sink. Adding in the fact that I was homeless, I was quickly on the verge of tears. I wiped my tears away and straightened my outfit before unlocking the door and stepping out into the diner.

Junie watched me, her eyes sad, as she made coffee. I gave her a small smile before disappearing into the back room and shoving my purse inside my locker.

When I reemerged, she was nowhere to be seen. The diner door dinged, and two men stepped into the room.

I smiled warmly as I walked over to them. "Two?" I asked.

They nodded, and I grabbed two menus.

I motioned for them to follow me. "This way, please."

I led them to a table in my area and handed each one a menu. After taking their drink orders, I headed over to the coffee pots to fill them and returned to their table. Once they placed their orders, I handed them to John, our cook.

Junie finally appeared a few minutes later. She led a young couple to a table on her side and got them their drinks. I passed by her as I was delivering food to the two men at my table, but she refused to look at me. I frowned but said nothing.

The diner grew busy after that, but it wasn't so busy that I didn't notice the way Junie was avoiding me. By lunchtime, I was seething. I had no idea what I'd done to upset her, but she was obviously mad at me. Normally, we would chat when we had time, but today, she was making sure to stay away from me.

I was relieved when my shift was finally over. As I was leaving the back room, Bob caught me.

He stuck his head out of his office and motioned me over. "Can I have a word with you?"

"Um…sure," I said as I walked into his office.

I had no idea what he wanted to talk to me about. I thought about the customers I'd had this morning. None of them had seemed upset, so I doubted if they'd complained about me.

"What's up?" I asked once I sat down in the chair across from his.

"Is everything okay with you, Claire?" he asked as he sat down.

"Yeah, why?"

He wrung his hands together, obviously uncomfortable. "Well, I talked to Junie this morning, and she's worried about you."

My mouth dropped open in surprise. I quickly changed from surprise to anger. I'd trusted Junie, and she'd sold me out. It was no wonder she'd been ignoring me all day.

"Look, I have no clue what she told you, but I'm fine. I promise."

"So, you're not sleeping in your car and using the restroom as your own personal shower?"

I looked away as shame filled me. "I promise you, I'm fine. I've hit a rough patch, but I'm working on it. I'm trying to save money, so I can get an apartment."

He sighed. "Why didn't you come to me, Claire? You know I'll help you."

I glanced up at him. "I don't need help, Bob. I'm fine. I'm used to looking out for myself."

"So, you won't let me give you money to get an apartment?"

"That really means a lot, Bob, but I won't let you do it. You're a great boss, and you've always been kind to me, but my life is my problem."

"I can't let you live in your car, Claire. I just can't. What if someone mugs you or worse? It isn't safe for a young girl to stay in a parking lot alone in the middle of the night. If you won't let me help you find an apartment, at least let me do *something*. I own the gym a few buildings down. It's within walking distance from here. The locker rooms have showers, and I have an office with a couch. I want you to stay there."

I shook my head. "I'm okay, Bob. I already have a hundred bucks saved up. I'll have an apartment in no time."

"Then, stay at the gym until then. Please, Claire. I'll worry about you if I know you're still sleeping in your car."

I hesitated. It would be nice to take an actual shower and have a safe place to stay at night. My car wasn't exactly the most comfortable thing in the world.

"I don't know, Bob," I said, feeling conflicted.

"I want you to stay at the gym. I won't take no for an answer, so you might as well save yourself the trouble and agree to stay." He frowned at me from across the desk.

"Fine," I said. "I'll stay at the gym, but I want to at least pay you something."

He shook his head. "You work your butt off here. Truthfully, you're one of the best employees I've ever had. You're staying for free."

"Thank you. I really appreciate this."

"You're welcome." He opened his desk drawer and pulled something out. "Take this pass over to the gym. They'll let you in. My office is on the second floor. I'll call over and have them show you where its at. Get settled in, take a shower, and relax. You deserve it."

Tears welled up in my eyes. I had no idea what I'd done to deserve a boss like Bob, but I wasn't complaining. I took the gym pass from him and shoved it in my pocket. After another quick thank-you, I left his office and hurried outside. I walked past my car and down the street to his gym.

When I entered, a young girl stood at the reception desk, talking on the phone.

"She just walked in. I'll take care of it." She hung up and smiled at me. "You must be Claire. I'm Sam. I'll show you where Bob's office is."

She grabbed a set of keys and walked through the gym. I looked around to see several exercise machines occupied by men and women. They paid us no attention as we passed them. We reached a set of stairs that I wouldn't have noticed if I'd been by myself, and we walked up to the next floor. At the top was a single wooden door.

Sam unlocked the door and held it open. "Here you go. If you need anything, just let me know. Oh, and here's the key. Bob said he'd drop off another one for me." She pulled a key off the key ring and handed it to me.

"Thank you." I entered the office and looked around.

"You're welcome. I'll leave you to get settled in." She closed the door behind her.

The office was bigger than I'd expected. A large desk sat across the room. Just like Bob's desk at the diner, it was covered in papers. A leather couch was against the left wall, and I made a mental note to purchase a sheet to put over it. A television was directly across from it on the right wall. Below the television sat a stand that had a microwave on the top shelf and a tiny refrigerator on the bottom shelf. I clapped my hands together in excitement. I could buy cheap TV dinners and noodles to eat for dinner. Neither would be much better than the fast food I'd been living off of, but it was nice to know I had options.

A door was behind the desk. I walked over and opened it to see a small bathroom. It didn't have a shower, but Bob had told me that I could shower downstairs in the locker room.

I moved across the room and plopped down on the couch. I smiled. For the first time in days, I had hope. Things were far from perfect, but this was a step in the right direction.

My next goal was to get everything legal on my car, so I wouldn't have to worry about my car being towed and getting stuck with a bunch of fines. After that, I would start looking for cheap apartments nearby. Hopefully, I'd have enough money saved up to rent one of them. I made a mental note to ask Bob if I could pick up extra hours at work.

I stood, wincing as my legs stuck to the couch. *Yeah, I definitely need to buy a sheet.* I dug through my purse to find my keys and added Bob's office key to my key ring so that I wouldn't lose it. That would be my luck.

I locked up the office, tossed my keys back into my purse, and headed downstairs. I gave Sam a smile as I passed by the front desk and walked outside.

I walked a few blocks to the dollar store and went inside. After grabbing a cart, I headed for the bedding aisle first and grabbed a sheet, a thin blanket, and a pillow. After shoving them in my cart, I walked over to the personal care items and stocked up on those as well. I also picked up two small tote bags—one to take with me when I showered at the gym and the other to shove my dirty clothes in. It would be easier to carry a bag around instead of my suitcase. I also got a few bottles of water, a few noodle cups, and a box of Pop-Tarts.

After paying for everything, I walked back to the diner parking lot and unlocked the trunk of my car. I threw my dirty clothes along with the sheet, blanket, and a clean pair of clothes into my new tote bag.

I ran inside the diner and changed in the restroom before heading to the Laundromat. I threw all the dirty laundry into the washer. I was sure most women would have looked at me in horror for mixing whites with colors, but I didn't want to spend the extra money on two separate washes. While I waited for my clothes to wash and then dry, I relaxed in a chair and read one of the books I'd borrowed from the library.

Once everything was dry and folded in my tote bag, I headed back to my car. I grabbed my suitcase from the trunk and wheeled it down to the gym. Getting it up the stairs to Bob's office was a pain, but I didn't complain once. I knew how much I owed Bob. Things were looking up, and I wasn't about to whine about trivial things.

I stashed all my belongings in the corner next to the couch. I laid the sheet out on the couch and then threw the blanket and pillow on top of it. Once I was satisfied with my new bed, I sat down and looked around the office. It was still early, and I hated to go to bed just yet, especially since I wasn't scheduled to work the next day.

I stood and looked out the door window to the gym below. I didn't think that Bob would mind if I worked out at the gym while I was staying here. I bit my lip as I debated on whether or not to go down. The gym wasn't super busy at the moment, so I wouldn't have to worry about making a complete fool of myself. I could use the exercise to tone up a bit. I wasn't fat by any means since Rick had made sure that we had just enough to eat.

Decision made, I walked over to my suitcase and pulled out a pair of plain black shorts and a tank top. After changing quickly, I headed downstairs. Once I reached the bottom, I wasn't sure which way to go. The only thing I knew about exercise was what I'd been forced to do in gym class in high school. It wasn't like any of my foster parents would have coughed up enough cash for me to join a gym.

"Are you lost?" a voice asked from behind me.

I spun around to see a man standing a few feet away.

I clutched my chest as I willed my heartbeat to settle. "You scared me to death."

"I'm sorry. I didn't mean to startle you. I just saw you standing here, looking around, and I thought you might need some help."

"It's okay," I said, feeling stupid for my outburst.

He smiled at me. "Is this your first day here?"

I nodded. "Yeah. Is it that obvious?"

"Just a little. If you're not sure where to start, why don't you join me on the treadmills for a bit?"

I studied him for a moment before nodding. "Sounds good to me."

He was older than me by several years. If I had to guess, I would say he was either in his late thirties or early forties. Our age difference didn't stop me from noticing just how attractive he was though. His hair was mostly brown with only a tiny amount of gray around his temples. His eyes were a rich chocolate brown. He had a few laugh lines, but it wasn't so much that they aged him. If anything, they added to his attractiveness.

As I watched him walk toward the treadmills, I noticed that he was also extremely fit. I blushed as I realized that I was checking out a man who was probably twice my age.

"Here we go." He stopped in front of two unoccupied treadmills sitting side by side.

He stepped up onto one as I stepped onto the other. I started my machine, making sure to keep it on a setting that would let me walk. It had been a while since my body saw any kind of exercise—unless I counted waitressing—and I didn't want to pull something.

I stared straight ahead, wishing that I could afford an iPod, like most of the people around me had. I wasn't good with small talk, and I was pretty sure I would blush if the man beside me tried to speak to me again, especially after I had checked him out.

"So, what's your name?" he asked.

I looked over to see him watching me. "Claire Reynolds."

"It's nice to meet you, Claire. I'm Robert Evans."

"Um…likewise." I looked away.

He chuckled. "You're not much for small talk, are you?"

I laughed nervously. "Is it that obvious?"

"A little bit. I'm sorry if I'm making you uncomfortable. I can leave if you'd like."

"No, it's okay. I'm just not good with strangers," I said.

"Well, you know my name now, so technically, I'm not a stranger."

"I guess that's true," I said thoughtfully.

"Why don't I tell you a little about myself? Then, if you're comfortable, you can tell me something about yourself as well."

I shrugged. "Okay."

He smiled. "All right then. Let's see…I'm forty-two. I love Chinese food. I live a few miles away from here in the new housing development. I'm a lawyer. I have a son named Cooper, and I'm also a widower. I lost my wife in a car accident last year."

"Oh my God, I'm so sorry, Robert. I can't even imagine," I said, feeling horrible for him.

"It's all right. It took me a long time to come to terms with Marie's death, but I'm trying to move on. My son has had a much harder time with it. He was very close to his mother."

I imagined a tiny version of Robert running around his house, searching for his mother. It reminded me of my first few years in foster care when I'd kept waiting for my mom to reappear and take me away.

"I lost my mom when I was little. My dad wasn't around, so I spent pretty much all my life in foster care," I said.

"That's rough. I've seen some really messed-up cases when it comes to foster parents. I can't imagine being a part of the system."

I shrugged. "They weren't all bad. I mean, yeah, a few were pretty bad, but most of the families took care of me."

"Are you out of the system now? I'm not trying to be nosy. It's just that you seem very young."

"You're not being nosy. I just turned eighteen a few days ago, so I'm out of the system now."

"Well, congratulations! You must be glad to be on your own."

I shrugged again. "Yeah, it's okay I guess. I'm still getting used to it."

"What are your plans now? Will you be attending WVU?"

"Probably not—at least, not right now. At the moment, I'm just trying to get settled and save up some cash," I said, not wanting to say any more.

Robert seemed like a really nice guy. Plus, he had to be loaded if he was a lawyer. I didn't want to admit that I was practically homeless and barely hanging on.

"Understandable. This world can be very cruel." He paused. "You said your birthday was the other day?"

"Yeah."

"Did you do anything to celebrate?"

I shook my head. "Nah, I was too busy working."

"That's unacceptable. You turn eighteen only once."

"It's not a big deal. Honest."

He frowned. "It is a big deal. Listen, why don't we celebrate? I don't know about you, but I could go for some cake."

I grinned. "Well, the place I work at has awesome chocolate cake."

"Then, it's settled." He pushed the stop button on his treadmill. "Go take a shower, and then meet me by the front door. We'll go have cake."

If his smile hadn't been so genuine, I would've said no. I knew next to nothing about this man, but he seemed so sincere. Besides, it would be nice to pretend that I had a friend, even for one night.

"All right." I stopped my treadmill as well.

"I'll see you in a few." He walked toward the locker rooms.

Once he disappeared inside the men's room, I turned and hurried up to Bob's office. I didn't bother with showering since I hadn't even broken a sweat on the treadmills. I dug through my clothes until I found a pair of jeans that didn't have holes. I took off my gym clothes and then pulled on my jeans and a plain blue T-shirt. I ran a brush through my hair and then headed back downstairs in record time. I didn't want him to see me coming out of Bob's office. Robert would ask questions that I didn't want to answer.

I waited by the front doors for a few minutes before Robert finally emerged from the men's locker room. My mouth dropped open in shock as I stared at him. He'd looked wonderful in his gym shorts and a plain T-shirt, but he was out of this world in the business suit he was now wearing. I couldn't imagine wearing a suit after going to the gym, but it must have been the norm for him. I looked down at my faded jeans and T-shirt, and I suddenly felt plain and poor. I had no doubt that his suit cost more than I could make in a month at the diner.

"Ready to go?" he asked.

"Yeah. The diner is nearby, so we can just walk."

He nodded as he held the door open for me.

The walk to the diner was quiet. Neither of us said much as we made our way down the almost empty street. It was after ten at night, and most places—with the exception of the diner and the gym— were closed already. When we reached the diner, I was hit with nerves so suddenly that I clutched my stomach. Robert was nice, but I was afraid that he'd look down on me for where I worked. The diner itself was nice, but we both knew that waitresses didn't usually make that much. It was common knowledge that most waitresses were flat broke.

"Are you okay?" His brow furrowed with concern.

"Yeah, I'm fine." I opened the door and walked inside.

Sarah and Stacey were working tonight. I waved at both of them as I led Robert to a table. Sarah approached, her eyes wide as she took in Robert. I looked away from Sarah and Stacey to keep from grinning. I knew what they must have been thinking.

"Hey, Claire. I didn't expect to see you here," Sarah said when she finally reached our table.

I smiled. "I was hoping we could get a couple pieces of the chocolate cake before you closed."

"Definitely." She looked between Robert and me. "Do you want anything else?"

"Can I have a glass of water as well?" Robert asked.

"Certainly. You want a Coke, Claire?" Sarah asked.

"Yes, please."

"Great. I'll be back in just a second." She turned and left, leaving me alone with Robert.

I studied the red-and-white checker tablecloth as I tried to think of something to say. I doubted if Robert was used to eating in a place like this. He probably always went to five-star restaurants.

"I like this place. It's cute," he said, breaking the silence.

I looked up to see him watching me. "Yeah, it's a nice place to work. Everyone is really great to me here, especially my boss, Bob."

"How long have you worked here?"

"Um…for a while. I just went full-time a couple of weeks ago after I graduated."

"I couldn't imagine working with the public face-to-face. I have a hard enough time dealing with the people I'm forced to see in court."

I laughed. "What? You're not a people person? That surprises me. You didn't have any trouble talking to me."

He grinned. "Well, you didn't seem too bad when I saw you standing there looking lost. Plus, you're a lot prettier than most of the judges and lawyers I have to deal with."

I blushed. "Well, thanks, I think."

He continued to watch me, causing my blush to creep down to my neck. I almost kissed Sarah when she arrived with our drinks and pieces of cake, drawing his attention away from me to her.

"Here you go. If you guys need anything, let me know," Sarah said.

When Robert looked away, she questioningly raised an eyebrow at me. I shook my head, hoping that she'd take the hint and not say anything. She grinned at me before walking away.

"Sorry that you don't have a candle on yours," Robert said.

"It's okay. Thank you for doing this for me."

"No thanks needed. Now, eat your cake."

I picked up my fork and attacked the cake in front of me. I almost moaned as the chocolate hit my tongue. No matter how long I lived, no one's cake could compare to Bob's. It was a secret recipe of his mother's, and I'd offered my right arm more than once in exchange for the recipe.

"Holy crap. This is so good," I said.

I looked up to see Robert watching me with a grin on his face.

"I can tell just by the look on your face," he said.

"Try it." I motioned to the piece in front of him. I watched as he took a bite. I almost laughed at the expression on his face. "Told you."

"You weren't kidding. Wow."

We sat together and chatted about unimportant things until it was time for the diner to close. I tried to pay for my cake, but he refused to let me.

"It's your birthday present from me."

"Thank you," I said, touched by his kindness.

Once our bill was paid, I said good night to the girls and walked with Robert back to the gym. We stopped outside.

"Do you need a ride home?" he asked.

I shook my head. "No, I live nearby. Thank you for tonight though. It's been a long time since I've met someone as nice as you."

"It was a pleasure spending the evening with you, Claire. Hopefully, we'll meet again."

I was shocked when he took my hand and pressed his lips to it.

"Um…yeah. Sure."

I waited until he left to walk back into the gym. I couldn't keep the smile off my face. Today had been a welcome surprise. After years of dealing with mostly cruel foster parents, it was good to see that some kind souls were still around.

I took a quick shower before settling down on Bob's couch. I fell asleep with a smile on my face for the first time in a long time.

The following week was uneventful.

I'd spent my only day off lounging on Bob's couch, watching television and eating noodles out of a cup. The rest of the week, I'd spent mostly at work. I had managed to make it to the DMV to get my car legalized. It had taken me three trips to bring everything I needed, and by the time I'd finally left the office, I had been ready to pull my hair out. I wished unspeakable pain on the three DMV workers I'd dealt with for putting me through so much crap just to get my car street legal.

I'd also opened up a bank account. The pride I'd felt when they handed me my paperwork was indescribable. My account barely had over a hundred dollars, but it was a start. I'd been saving up every penny I could, so I would be able to make another deposit when I got paid.

No one at the gym had seemed to notice that I was staying in Bob's office, except for Sam. She would check in on me from time to time just to make sure that I was doing okay. Occasionally, I'd walk to the front desk when she was working. I enjoyed chatting with her, and I would look forward to it on the days she worked. Bob had stopped in a couple of times to do paperwork, but he hadn't stayed too long. I'd almost laughed when he told me that he didn't want to intrude. After all, it was *his* office.

Work had been hectic, but I'd considered it a blessing. The busier we were, the more tips I would make. Sarah had asked me endless questions about Robert, but I'd brushed them aside. She'd assumed that I was on a date. The thought itself had made me laugh.

Robert and I were on two different social levels. Also, his age was a good indication that he had just been nice to me. Men like him wouldn't look at me that way. After learning that I worked as a waitress, he'd probably felt sorry for me. That was why he'd paid for my birthday cake. He'd pitied me. The thought had bothered me, but I'd pushed it away. If he had known I was living in a gym, he probably never would have spoken to me to begin with.

By the end of the week, I'd convinced myself that Robert had only paid attention to me because he felt sorry for me. So, when he walked into the diner that evening, I nearly fell over in shock. He searched the room until he found me. I stood frozen as he bypassed Junie and headed straight for me.

"Claire, we meet again," he said as he stopped in front of me.

"Robert, what a surprise." I pulled myself from my stupor. "What are you doing here?"

"Well, I met this waitress the other day, and she spoke highly of this place. I thought I'd stop by and have dinner."

Shocked by his answer, I tried to think of something to say. "Oh…well, I'm glad you stopped in." I gestured to where my tables were. "Why don't you have a seat over there? I'll bring you a menu."

"Perfect." He turned and walked over to one of my tables.

I hurried to the front and picked up a menu from the pile.

Junie grabbed my arm and pulled me back. "Is that the guy Sarah was giving you a hard time about?"

"Yeah. His name is Robert. I met him at Bob's gym."

She studied him carefully, a frown forming on her face. "Be careful, Claire. He's a lot older than you."

I laughed. "He's not proposing marriage, Junie. Don't worry about me."

Her frown only deepened. "I don't care. Men like that are after one thing, and you're a pretty young girl. I don't want you to get hurt."

It was my turn to frown. "Seriously, Junie, chill out. Nothing's going on."

She nodded as she said, "For your sake, I hope not." With that, she turned and headed toward her tables.

I forced the frown off my face as I walked over to Robert's table. "Here you go." I laid the menu in front of him and pulled out my pen and pad of paper I used to take orders. "Would you like something to drink?"

"I'll have a water."

"Great. I'll be right back." I hurried away to grab his water.

When I returned, he was still staring at his menu.

"Are you ready to order? Or do you need more time?"

"I can't decide what I want. What do you suggest?"

"Well, the chicken and dumplings are really good."

"Then, that's what I'll have." He closed his menu and handed it back to me.

"Perfect. I'll bring it out to you in just a few."

After I placed his order, I checked on my other tables. We had an hour until closing, and I only had three other tables to wait on. I took my time with each, making sure they had everything they needed. I knew I was avoiding Robert, but I couldn't help it. I never expected to see him again. Plus, Junie's concern was nagging at me, causing me to feel unsure of myself.

When our cook, John, rang the bell to let me know that Robert's order was ready, I forced myself to grow a backbone. I grabbed his food and carried it over to his table, determined not to let my uncertainty become a problem. He was a customer just like everyone else who walked through the front door.

"Everything look good? Do you need more water?" I asked, trying not to fidget as I stood next to him.

"It looks perfect, and I don't need anything at the moment." He smiled. "Unless you'd like to sit down with me while I eat."

I glanced around at my other tables. "I really can't. I'm on the clock."

He looked over his shoulder at the tables. "I think everyone is okay right now. Why don't you take a break?"

I bit my lip as I debated on what to do. My other tables were okay for the moment, and I doubted that Bob would care if I took a tiny break.

"All right, but just for a minute." I pulled out the chair across from him and sat down.

"So, how have you been?" He began to eat.

"Um…good. You?"

"Busy. I have two tough cases that I'm working on at once. I planned to stop by to visit you earlier in the week, but I've been swamped."

"Oh," I said, unsure of how to reply.

Something about this man made me feel like an idiotic fourteen-year-old. Maybe it was our age difference, or maybe it was the way he carried himself. He commanded the attention of everyone in the room. I, on the other hand, tried to hide from people in general.

"Relax, Claire. I'm not going to bite you." He smiled at me from across the table.

"Sorry. I guess I'm just surprised that you stopped by."

"What can I say? You left quite an impression on me the other night. I've been thinking about you a lot this past week."

I raised an eyebrow in surprise, but I said nothing.

"So, tell me what you've been up to since I last saw you."

"Not much really. I've been working a lot, trying to save up as much money as I can. I even went to the bank and opened an account." I regretted the words as soon as they'd left my mouth. I didn't want him to feel sorry for me because I didn't have money. Telling him that I'd opened my first bank account was stupid, too. I suddenly felt like a child.

"That's wonderful. I'm sure you're still getting used to being on your own. Saving money and putting it into an account is smart. When I turned eighteen, my father opened a bank account and put in five thousand dollars to get me started. That was the only money he gave me. He expected me to survive on my own while I was in college. I hated it at the time, but I understand why he did it. If people are given the easy way in life, that's what they'll always expect. Those who fight for everything they have respect it more."

I agreed with him. I'd survived with almost no help at all for most of my life. It'd changed me and made me realize how important it was to save every dime.

I tried to picture the man before me as an eighteen-year-old college student, but I couldn't. "What were you like when you were in college?"

He laughed. "I was a cocky little shit. I thought the world owed me everything, especially after the way my father had abandoned me financially. I also liked to party, which got me in trouble a time or two. It took me a few years to pull my head out of my ass and focus on what was important at the time—school. Once I did, I never looked back. I graduated and then moved on to law school."

"I can't picture you like that – in college and partying." I studied him.

He seemed so put together, not like someone who had been a rebellious teenager.

"I've changed a lot over the years. Time does that to a person."

"I guess so. I've never really been the partying type. I was too busy looking after the younger kids in my foster homes."

"Growing up in foster care is different from a normal family situation. You're an old soul, Claire. I think that's why I'm so drawn to you."

"You mean it's not because of my wonderful personality?" I joked.

"Well, it's that, too." He hesitated for a moment. "Claire, I was wondering if you'd like to have dinner with me one evening. I'd love to take you to my favorite restaurant in town."

I had no idea what to say. While I liked Robert and definitely found him attractive, we were two different people. I wasn't in his social class, not even close. Plus, he was so much older than me. A few years wouldn't have been an issue, but he was twenty-four years older. Hell, he was old enough to be my father.

My eyes widened in surprise. "Um…I don't know. I barely know you."

"I think dinner would be the perfect way to get to know each other. If you're uncomfortable with the thought of it being a date, it doesn't have to be."

"I don't really date. I don't have time," I said, still stalling.

His lips twitched. "Neither do I, but I'll make an exception for you, Claire. Something about you pulls me in. You're the first woman I've even noticed since my wife passed away."

I instantly felt guilty. The poor man had lost the love of his life. I couldn't imagine the pain he'd gone through after her death.

"I really don't have anything to wear."

I thought about the contents of my suitcase back at the gym. I had no idea where Robert would want to take me, but I doubted waitress uniforms and jeans with holes in the knees would be the standard dress code.

"I'll take care of that as well."

"You don't have to buy me clothes, Robert. I'm no one's charity case."

He frowned. "I don't think of you as charity, Claire. It's quite the opposite actually. I have a feeling that having you around will help me immensely."

"How do you figure that?"

"I could use a friend," he said simply.

I bit my lip as I debated on what to do. "All right, I'll have dinner with you."

The smile he gave me was worth taking the chance. I couldn't help but grin when I saw his expression turning from worried to relieved in just a few seconds.

"Excellent. Do you work tomorrow evening?"

I shook my head. "No, I have the morning shift. I get off at three."

"Perfect. What's your address? I'll have my car pick you up tomorrow."

I hesitated. "Why don't I just meet you here?"

He gave me a questioning look but nodded. "All right. I'll send the car for you tomorrow at five then." He pulled a fifty from his wallet and handed it to me as he stood. "Good night, Claire."

"Let me get your change before you leave," I said as I stood.

He waved me off. "Don't worry about it."

I watched him walk out of the diner with his money still clutched tightly in my hand. What had I gotten myself into?

"Claire, a man just dropped this off for you," Sarah said as I stepped out of the restroom.

I took the box from her and set it on the table next to me. "Did he say who it was from?"

"Nope. Hurry up and open it! I want to see what it is." She gestured to the box.

I laughed at her impatience. "I wonder what it is."

"Open it and see! Jesus, do you need directions?"

I stuck my tongue out at her as I untied the ribbon around the box. I cautiously lifted the lid, unsure of what I'd find inside. My eyes widened in surprise when they landed on a pair of pale blue heels. I lifted them carefully and noticed another box. I set the heels aside and opened the other box. I picked up a pale blue dress. It was gorgeous and far more expensive than anything I'd ever worn before. It was strapless with a ruched bodice. The skirt had hanging sashes all the way around it. I held the dress up against my chest, unable to believe that I was holding something so beautiful.

"Oh my God! Who bought you that?"

I looked at the tag and nearly fainted when I saw the designer's name. "Robert. I don't know anyone else who could afford a dress like this. Holy shit, Sarah. I don't even know what to say."

"Don't say anything. Go climb that man's body like a monkey and pray that he sends more shit like that!"

"Sarah!" I said, embarrassed by her words.

"What? If a guy sent me something like that, I wouldn't think twice about *thanking* him properly. You scored with this dude, Claire. Hot damn."

I shook my head. "I can't accept this. My God, it probably cost more than my car."

"You can and you will accept it. It's a gift, Claire. You can't just send it back. What the hell did you do for him to get you something like this?"

"Nothing, except agree to have dinner with him tonight."

"Marry him," Sarah deadpanned.

I laughed. "You're an idiot."

Sarah watched as I carefully placed the dress back in the box, and then I put the shoes in as well. I closed the lid, carried the box to the back room, and placed it in my locker. My thoughts were muddled with confusion as I debated on what to do. I was both mortified and flattered that Robert had bought something so expensive for me. I wanted to keep it, but I wasn't sure if I could.

I shook my head and walked back to the front of the diner. I would think about it and decide once my shift ended.

I can't believe I'm keeping it. I stared at myself in the full-length mirror of the gym dressing room.

After my shift, I'd hurried back to the gym to get ready for my date. After showering, shaving, and lathering every inch of my body with vanilla-scented lotion, I'd changed into the dress Robert had purchased for me. It fit perfectly. I couldn't help but smile at that. What were the odds of him knowing my exact size? After slipping into my matching heels, I'd sat in front of one of the mirrors and attacked my hair. I'd counted my blessings that the gym had outlets for my hair dryer and straightener. After making sure that my hair looked okay, I moved on to makeup. I had very little to choose from. I didn't wear makeup often, especially since money was so tight.

I had to admit that I looked good. The small amount of eyeliner I'd applied made my blue eyes pop. The dress clung to my tiny frame down to my waist before flaring out. The heels made my legs look longer than they were. I couldn't help but wonder what Robert would think when he saw me.

Once I was satisfied with my appearance, I headed over to the diner to wait on Robert's car. I took my time walking, afraid that I'd kill myself in my new shoes. I was used to my ratty old sneakers. I wobbled a few times, but I finally arrived at the diner without embarrassing myself.

When I walked in the front door, Junie was standing at one of the nearby tables. She glanced up at me before returning her attention to the customer she had been talking to. I watched as she froze and turned back to me with a look of shock on her face. She quickly excused herself and walked over to where I was standing.

"Claire?" she asked when she stopped in front of me.

I grinned. "Come on, Junie. I don't look *that* different."

"I can't…wow, you look amazing!"

"Thanks."

"I love that dress. Where did you get it from?"

"Uh…Robert gave it to me. I'm having dinner with him tonight."

Her expression instantly turned sour. "I should've known. Please listen to me, Claire. I don't know why, but something about that man bothers me. I want you to be careful."

"I will. I know you're still going to worry no matter what I say, but I really do think Robert is a good guy."

"Maybe you're right." She glanced behind me. "I'm betting that car is for you."

I turned to see a black Cadillac idling outside the front door. "Probably. Wish me luck."

Junie surprised me when she hugged me tightly. "You don't need luck, sweetheart." She released me and shoved me toward the door. "Just be careful."

I waved as I walked to the door, and then I stepped outside. An older man was standing next to the car. I walked over, unsure of whether or not this was my ride.

"Claire?" he asked.

"That's me," I said shyly.

"I'm supposed to take you to Mr. Evans." He opened the back door.

"Thank you." I slid into the backseat of the car.

He closed the door and walked around the front of the car. Once he was situated behind the wheel, he pulled out onto the main road. The ride across town was silent. I almost wished that he'd turned on the radio. Silence made me nervous.

I fidgeted as we crossed into the wealthier side of town. We pulled up to a restaurant I'd never heard of and stopped. The driver was out of the car and opening my door before I could even blink. I climbed out, careful not to trip over my heels, and stared up at the building.

"Mr. Evans is waiting for you inside." He closed my door.

"Thank you." I walked to the door and pulled it open.

The outside of the building was plain, nothing more than bricks, but the inside was another matter. I was in awe as I took in my surroundings. The diner was a hole-in-the-wall compared to this place. The floors were a black marble, and the walls were a deep red color. The restaurant was massive with four crystal chandeliers hanging from the ceiling.

"Can I help you?" a woman asked.

"Um…yes. I'm supposed to meet Robert Evans here."

"Of course. Follow me."

I hurried to keep up with her as she led me to the other side of the room. I noticed that she had no problem walking in her high-heeled shoes. I was instantly jealous of her. As we approached a table, I saw Robert smile as he stood.

"Claire, I'm so glad you could make it. You look beautiful." He hurried to help me sit down in a chair.

I was amazed as he pushed my chair in for me. I hadn't expected him to be so polite. Then again, this was Robert. Of course he was as polite as he was charismatic. I was so out of my league with him.

"Thanks. You look nice, too," I said.

As he sat back down, I drank him in without caring. He was wearing another suit tonight, one that had to have been tailored just to fit him. He looked strong and confident in it, something I wished I felt. Despite our age difference, I couldn't keep denying the fact that I was attracted to him.

"I was right. That dress looks gorgeous on you."

I gave him a weak smile. "I love it, but you didn't have to buy something like this for me. It's too much."

"Nonsense. It was worth every penny," he said as a waiter approached our table. "I already ordered for you. I hope that's okay."

Truthfully, it wasn't. I would rather have ordered for myself, but I didn't want to hurt his feelings by telling him so. As the waiter set my plate down in front of me, I decided that maybe it was a good idea that he'd ordered. I had no idea what I was about to eat.

"Um…what is it?" I asked, feeling like an idiot.

"It's grilled eggplant involtini. It has roasted tomatoes, capers, kalamata olives, Green Glades mozzarella, parmesan, and fontina barley risotto," the waiter said.

He reached for the cloth napkin sitting in a wine glass in front of me. I stared at him in shock as he unfolded the napkin and placed it on my lap.

Yep, I'm way out of my league here.

"Oh, okay," I said, trying not to be embarrassed. I still had no clue what I was about to eat, but I'd made enough of a fool of myself to ask for more of an explanation.

"Try it. If you don't like it, we can order something else for you." Robert took a drink from his wine glass.

I reached down for my fork, but then I stopped and stared in horror at the multiple forks, spoons, and knives sitting next to my plate. I had no idea which one to use. Feeling like a fool, I grabbed and picked up the fork on the outside along with one of the knives. I prayed they were the right ones.

I cut off a tiny bite of the eggplant. Hoping that it wouldn't taste horrible, I took a bite. I was pleasantly surprised when I liked it. "Wow, it is good."

"I thought you'd like it." He picked up his own fork.

I was relieved to see that he'd picked up the same one as me.

We ate in silence for a few minutes. I glanced around the room, taking in the other guests. Our table was in the corner, several feet away from the closest table. The people I saw were dressed similarly to Robert and me. Most of them were also wearing suits and dresses.

I stared down at my plate. I was terrified to know how much our dinners would cost Robert.

"So, I think we're supposed to get to know each other better over dinner," Robert said.

"That was the plan," I joked.

"Well then, tell me more about yourself."

"What do you want to know?" I asked.

"Anything. Everything. What's your favorite food? What annoys you? What are your hobbies?"

"Let's see…my favorite food is pizza for sure. People who talk too much annoy me. I don't really have any hobbies, except for reading. I love romance novels and paranormal books. I'm pretty sure the local librarian knows me on a first name basis at this point. I'm there once or twice a week. What about you?"

"I don't really have a favorite food, but if I had to choose, I'd probably go with steak. You can't go wrong there. As for what annoys me, most of the time, it's my coworkers and other lawyers. They're all so…full of themselves—I mean, the lawyers. I hate attending social functions with any of them, but it's a must in my line of work. I never know when I'll need a favor from one of them. I also like to travel. Actually, I just got back from a trip I took to London a few weeks ago."

"I've always wanted to visit there. I love history, and the entire country is just packed with it."

"I'll take you there sometime," Robert said.

"What? Oh no, I didn't mean that. I just think it would be cool to go explore. I'll never be able to afford a trip like that."

"You wouldn't have to pay for anything. I'd take you."

I glanced away, suddenly uncomfortable with where the conversation had gone. It seemed like it always came back to money—the fact that he had a lot of it, and I had almost none.

"Did I say something to upset you?" he asked.

"No…well, yes." I sighed. "I suppose I might as well say it now. Robert, I know you must have a lot of money. It's pretty obvious that I don't. When you say things like that, it makes me uncomfortable. It's embarrassing to spend time with someone like you when I'm dirt poor."

He frowned as he put his fork down. "Listen to me, Claire. I don't care how much money you have in your bank account. Truthfully, I never even really thought about whether or not you have money."

"You might not have considered it, but I have. I like you, Robert, but I don't want you to look down on me. Also, I don't want you to think that I'm spending time with you because you have money."

"I would never look down on you. I don't know you very well, but from what I can tell, you're not a gold digger. When I look at you, I see a beautiful young woman who's trying to get her life in order. Your kindness radiates around you like an aura. I would never assume you're trying to use me."

I bit my lip. *A beautiful young woman.* "I'm also a lot younger than you. Does that bother you?"

He shook his head. "It doesn't. The moment I laid eyes on you, I knew I had to get to know you. Yes, I'm older than you, but I'm not worried about it." He hesitated. "Unless it's going to be a problem for you."

"It's not a problem. It's just that we're in totally different places in our lives. You're so much more experienced in life than I am. I'm confused as to why you're interested in me. You have built a life for yourself, and I'm just starting. Spending time with me is like taking a step back."

"Quite the contrary, Claire. Spending time with you is refreshing. Did I ever expect to be attracted to someone so much younger? Definitely not, but I promise that I'm quite attracted to you. If it's not a problem for you, it's definitely not a problem for me."

I was flattered by his words, but my uneasiness wouldn't leave me. "I'm not even old enough to drink."

He laughed. "Well, there goes my plans to get you drunk and have my way with you."

I couldn't help but laugh with him. "I'm being silly. I know."

"Not at all. I think something great could come out of this if you give it a chance. You just have to put your doubts aside."

I thought carefully on what I was about to say. "I think you're right. I like you, Robert, but I could see myself falling for you fast. If we do this, I want us to take it slow. Is that okay with you?"

"Of course, Claire. I never want you to feel pressured."

I smiled. "All right then."

"Just so we're clear, this conversation is me staking my claim on you. If we're doing this, I don't want you seeing anyone else."

"Of course not! I'm not like that," I said, horrified he felt the need to clarify that to me.

"Good. I just want to make sure that we're on the same page."

As dinner progressed, I forced myself to relax. Now that we'd talked about the important things, our conversation turned light and playful. I laughed more over dinner than I had in a long time. Robert seemed to do that to me. I was always smiling or laughing when he was around. He made me happy.

My only concern was that he'd want to take me home at the end of the night. I didn't want to start our relationship with lies, but I couldn't bring myself to tell him the truth. Regardless of what he'd said, I was ashamed about my lack of money. If he knew that I was practically homeless, he might insist on helping me, and I wouldn't be able to handle that.

After we finished dinner and dessert, Robert paid the bill, and we left. He kept his hand on my lower back as we walked out of the restaurant and to his car. I smiled at the simple gesture. No one had ever paid attention to me the way Robert did.

Once we were in his car, he turned to me. "Do you want me to take you straight home or back to the diner?"

"Um…the diner. My car is parked there."

He opened his mouth to say something, but then he seemed to think better of it, and he nodded instead. While steering the car toward my work, he reached over and turned on the radio. I frowned as classical music began playing softly from the speakers. I wasn't a fan of classical, but I doubted that he'd appreciate if I asked him to change it to rock music. Something told me he wasn't a fan of rock or heavy metal music like I was. I grinned at the thought of him listening to Korn, Crossfaith, or even Pop Evil.

I looked around the inside of Robert's car. The interior was spectacular, especially when I compared it to my car. The seats were leather and heated. His steering wheel had controls all over it. I couldn't even begin to guess what they were for. My car was so old that it had a tape player in it. His had a CD player and a large screen with different options all over it. My fingers itched to touch the screen and see what kind of technology was on it, but I held back. His car was exactly like him—luxurious and expensive. I almost snorted when I thought about my car. It was just like me—worn-out and barely holding on.

We pulled into the diner parking lot, and he shut off the car.

"Where's your car?" he asked.

I pointed to my poor car where it was parked on the far side of the lot. "Over there."

He frowned. "Oh…wow."

I chuckled. "It's a clunker, I know, but it gets me to where I need to go."

"It's very…colorful."

"I call it my Christmas car since it's red and green."

He laughed. "Please tell me someone didn't buy it as a Christmas present for you."

"Like any of my foster parents would buy me anything like that."
I snorted. "I saved every penny I could, so I could buy a car. Have
you ever tried to ride the bus around Morgantown? It's not fun,
especially if you want to be on time."

"Truthfully, I'd be more afraid of your car breaking down than
taking the bus."

I shrugged. "It has once or twice, but luckily, the repairs weren't
horrible."

"Claire, you're probably not going to like what I'm about to say,
but I'm going to say it anyway. I'm not comfortable with you driving
that car. I want you to use one of mine until you can save up for one
that's not quite so…unstable."

He was right. I wasn't happy with that. Warning bells went off in
my head. He was moving way too fast.

"No way, Robert. You're not letting me borrow one of your
cars!"

"Yes, I am. You can argue all you want, but I'm not giving in.
Now that I know what you're driving, I'll worry about you constantly.
Come on, it looks like it's going to fall apart!"

I glared at him. "I'm *not* agreeing to this. If you try to give me one
of yours, I won't drive it. I'm not kidding."

"Claire—"

"No."

He sighed. "Will you at least think about it?"

"I'll tell you what. If my car ever breaks down to the point where it's no longer repairable, you can get me a cheap car. Until then, I'm driving mine."

He frowned but finally nodded. "I'm only agreeing because I don't want to fight with you."

"That's fine with me, but you're not going to guilt me into taking you up on your offer."

I couldn't believe he'd even suggested something like that. I'd known the man existed for only a week, and I'd been on only one date with him. If we'd been together for months, I might have agreed but definitely not after one date.

"I should probably head home," I said finally.

"Good night, Claire." He reached across the console and cupped my cheek. "If you won't let me buy you a car, can I at least kiss you good night?"

I smiled. "I can handle that."

He pulled my face closer to his and gently kissed my lips. I sighed at the contact. It was nice. He continued to kiss me for a few more seconds before releasing me. I frowned when I realized I hadn't seen stars like the girls did in my romance novels. I shook my head to clear it. That was a stupid thought. My books were fiction. Those things didn't happen in real life.

"Good night." I climbed out of the car and walked to my own.

Robert waited until I was in my car before he pulled away. I waited a few minutes to make sure he was really gone before climbing back out. I thought about our night as I walked to the gym. It had been nice, like our kiss. Being the perfect gentleman, Robert had been kind to me. I just hoped I wasn't making a mistake by agreeing to this relationship.

The next morning, I headed to the library to return the books I'd borrowed a few days before. I dropped my books off in the return bin and walked to the paranormal section. As I searched through the shelves, I sighed. I'd been coming to this library for almost a year, and I'd read pretty much everything they had in paranormal books and over half of their romance collection.

After finding a book that looked halfway interesting, I walked over to one of the tables and sat down. I didn't have to be at work until later, and I didn't have anywhere else I needed to be, so I figured reading in the library would be the best place.

After two chapters in, I gave up. It wasn't the book's fault. I just couldn't concentrate today. I kept thinking about my date with Robert. I was still kind of ticked over the fact that he'd tried to give me a car. I would need to set boundaries with him before we went any further. I wouldn't mind if he bought me small things occasionally, but the expensive dress and the car offer was way too much and way too fast.

Other than the car conversation, last night had been perfect. I smiled as I thought about the way he'd kissed me—sweet and gentle. That was a good sign. If he'd tried to paw me to death in his car, I probably would've run and never looked back. I just needed time to process the fact that I was with someone like him.

I'd never really thought about my future before. I hadn't had the time. Now though, it was definitely something I thought about. If things went well with Robert and we ended up together permanently, my life would be so much easier. I'd never have to worry about working overtime or how I was going to afford rent. Robert hit me as the type who took care of others, and without a doubt, I knew that he would make sure I was taken care of.

I didn't want to be one of those women who needed a man to take care of everything. I was stronger than that, but as I sat in the library and stared at the shelves around me, I let myself have a moment of weakness. I just wanted to be taken care of. I wanted someone else to handle all my problems. I'd taken care of others my entire life. Would it be so horrible if someone took care of me?

My eyes landed on the row of ancient computers across the room. I bit my lip as I debated on what to do. Besides the fact that Robert had a son and was a lawyer, I knew next to nothing about him. Surely, there would be news articles about him and the cases he'd worked on. I might even find something about his wife.

I stood and walked over to where the librarian was sitting.

She glanced up and smiled at me. "What can I do for you, Claire?"

I almost laughed over the fact that she did know my name. "I was wondering if I could use one of your computers."

"Of course. It's five dollars for an hour of use. If you need to print something, it's twenty cents a sheet."

I dug through my purse until I found a five. I handed it over to her. "Thanks!"

"You're welcome. If you need any help, let me know."

"I will," I called over my shoulder as I walked to the row of computers.

I sat down at the one farthest away from her. I giggled over the note that said users would lose their library cards and have to pay a small fine if they looked at adult sites.

Once I was logged in, I pulled up the Internet browser and searched for Robert's name. I'd expected to see a few hits but nothing like what came up. I stared in shock as article after article about him appeared.

I clicked on the first one, dated almost a year ago, and read through it. Robert had managed to win a high-profile case between his client and the local police department. The amount his client had received wasn't specified, but the article made it clear that they knew it had been a lot. I closed out of that article and pulled up the next one. It was another high-profile case, but this one was between a city worker and the city. Robert had won that one as well. After reading several more articles, one thing became clear. Robert never lost a case.

Further down the page, I found an article on his wife's sudden death. Tears welled up in my eyes as I read it.

Robert Evans, high-profile defense attorney, lost his wife in a tragic car accident Tuesday night. His wife, Marie Evans, was struck by an oncoming car.

She lost control of her vehicle and struck an embankment. Mrs. Evans was pronounced dead on the scene.

She leaves behind her husband, Robert, and one son, Cooper. Mrs. Evans was on several committees in Morgantown and organized the local children's shelter. In lieu of flowers, the Evans family is asking that donations be made in her honor to the children's shelter.

Mr. Evans issued a statement requesting that the press be respectful as he and his family mourn the loss of their loved one. Authorities are still searching for the other vehicle involved in the collision. If you have any information, please contact the Morgantown Police Department.

I wiped the tears from my cheeks as I closed out of the article. I knew what it felt like to have someone ripped out of your life like that. Even worse, the person responsible for her death had never been arrested as far as I could tell. That alone must have driven Robert mad. I didn't know how old Cooper had been, but I imagined he'd suffered greatly over the loss of his mother. I'd been so young when I lost my mother, and I still felt the pain from her death.

Another thought struck me. If my relationship with Robert became serious, he would want to introduce me to his son. Oh God, Cooper would probably hate me, thinking that I was trying to replace his mother. I vowed to myself that if I ever did meet him, I would let him know that I wasn't trying to replace her in any way.

I pulled up a few more articles on Robert, trying to distract myself from Marie's death. I was shocked when I noticed a photo of Robert with the state governor. I couldn't believe that my boyfriend was the man in this photo. I had known he was a lawyer, but I hadn't realized just how big he was. In my defense, reading the newspaper hadn't exactly been at the top of my to-do list.

I closed the search window and logged out of the computer. I could have looked at more articles, but I knew they'd say the same things the others had. Robert was a big deal.

After checking out my book, I headed toward the diner. It was hot out today, but I didn't mind. As I walked down the street, I looked in the windows of a few stores, wishing I had enough money to afford some of the clothes hanging up on display. One day, I would be able to, but until then, I just had to keep saving. Even though Robert was in my life now, that didn't mean that my plans had changed. Right now, my top priority was saving enough money for an apartment. Once I did that, I'd look into the tuition rates at WVU and go from there. I knew it would be a while before I was ready for that.

Sarah was working when I walked into the diner.

"Hey! Someone dropped off a package for you early this morning. I put it in front of your locker," she called as she carried a tray of food past me.

"Another one?" I asked, surprised.

"Yep. It's not as big as the other one though."

I frowned as I walked to the back room. When I stopped in front of my locker, I saw a small package on the bottom. I picked it up and studied it. Whatever it was, it couldn't be another dress. The package was way too small for that. It was around the size of a book. I opened it slowly, almost afraid to know what was inside. As soon as the wrapping paper was gone, I smiled. It was an e-reader. On our date last night, I had mentioned my love of reading, and he'd bought me this. I lifted it out of the box and noticed a gift card and note. My eyes widened as I took in the amount of the gift card. I could buy a ton of books with a hundred dollars. I set the e-reader and gift card aside and grabbed the note.

CLAIRE,

I HOPE YOU ENJOY YOUR GIFT. IF YOU NEED MORE BOOKS ONCE YOU'VE SPENT YOUR GIFT CARD, LET ME KNOW. I HOPE YOU'LL FORGIVE ME FOR LAST NIGHT. IT WASN'T MY PLACE TO OFFER TO LET YOU BORROW ONE OF MY CARS. I HOPE YOU'RE NOT ANGRY WITH ME. PLEASE CALL ME WHEN YOU GET A CHANCE.

SINCERELY,

ROBERT

He left his number on the bottom of the note. I hadn't even thought about the fact that I hadn't had his number. I didn't know what I'd do when he asked me for mine. There was no way I could afford a cell phone, not even one of those cheap ones.

I smiled as I put everything back in the box. While I wasn't happy that he was spending money on me, I could accept an e-reader and a gift card. They had definitely cost less than a car.

Ten minutes later, I was still smiling when I walked back out into the diner.

Sarah cornered me the minute she saw me. "So? What was it?"

"An e-reader and a gift card."

She grinned. "He's so sweet, and he obviously has it bad for you if he's dropping cash on you like that."

I shrugged. "We agreed to take it slow. We'll see where it goes."

She snorted. "Buying you presents before and after one date isn't slow. Mark my words—you'll be married to him in less than a year."

I frowned. "I doubt that. I just don't understand why he's so interested in me. I'm nothing special."

"Are you kidding me? You're a bombshell, Claire. Every guy who walks through the door looks at you. Have you looked at yourself in the mirror lately? Blonde hair, blue eyes, tiny waist, and nice boobs—you have it all. If I wasn't straight, I'd so tap that."

I burst out laughing. "Oh my God, Sarah. I never know what's going to come out of your mouth next!"

She grinned. "Hey, I only speak the truth. Look, I know you haven't had the easiest life, but you need to accept the fact that you're attractive. I'm aware that none of your foster parents were nice enough to tell you that, but I will. Get some self-confidence, chick. You need to stop being so hard on yourself."

By the end of my shift, I was exhausted. I walked to the back room and grabbed my things before leaving the diner through the employee exit. I stopped short when I saw a man leaning against my car. Fear seized me until I recognized it was Robert.

I walked toward him. "Robert? What are you doing here?"

He smiled. "I just left my office, and I thought I'd swing by since I haven't heard from you. You did get my note, didn't you?"

"Oh, yeah. Sorry I didn't call you. We've been busy all night." I hesitated. "Plus, I don't have a phone to call you with."

I was surprised when I saw anger flash across his face. It was gone a second later, making me wonder if I'd just imagined it.

"Let me make sure I understand this right. Your car isn't very reliable, and you have no cell phone, right? So, if your car did break down, you wouldn't even be able to call anyone?"

I glanced at my feet, embarrassed. "Yeah, you got it right."

He sighed before reaching out and pulling me against him. "What am I going to do with you, Claire? Why don't you have a cell phone?"

I relaxed against his chest, and he rested his chin on top of my head.

"Because I can't afford one. I'm working on it though, okay? As soon as I have one, I'll give you the number."

"Try to get it soon, or I'm going to drive myself nuts while wondering if you're all right."

"I will, I promise," I said.

I listened to his heartbeat. It was strong and even. Being this close to him calmed me. It was nice to have someone who genuinely cared if I was okay or not. Besides Junie and Bob, I couldn't think of anyone who would worry about me.

"By the way, thank you for the gift. I love it," I said.

"I thought you would. If you run out of money to buy books, let me know, and I'll get you another card."

I nodded even though I would never ask him after spending the gift card. "Okay."

We stood together in the parking lot for a few minutes before he finally pulled away. "I need to head home. I have to be in court early tomorrow."

I stepped away from him and smiled. "All right, I'll see you later. Thanks for stopping by to visit me."

"I thought about you all day. You're starting to drive me nuts but in a good way." He pulled me close again and gently kissed me. "Do you have to work tomorrow night?"

"No, I'm on the morning shift tomorrow."

"Good. I want to take you out for dinner. You choose where you want to go."

I was all for that plan. Anywhere I'd want to go wouldn't have a dress code. "Sounds good to me."

He waved and then headed for his car. I watched him pull away. Once his taillights disappeared, I started walking toward the gym. I couldn't wait for tomorrow night.

Five Weeks Later

Robert held my hand as we walked out of the movie theater together. I shifted closer, and he wrapped his arm around me. I rested my head against his chest as we approached his car. Once we were inside, he took my hand and held it as he steered us toward the diner.

"Tonight was fun," I said as I looked over at him.

"Yeah, it was. It's been a long time since I went to the theater to see a movie. I needed tonight."

"Me, too." I relaxed further into my seat. "I'm so tired. I've been working doubles at the diner. I can't complain though. I'm saving a lot of money."

"Good, so you can get a cell phone now." Robert glanced over at me.

I sighed. "Yes, I'll buy one soon. I just hate spending money on one."

"I tried to add you to my plan, but you wouldn't let me," he grumbled.

"And I still won't let you. I'll buy a cheap throwaway one. It's not like I'm going to talk to anyone besides you," I said stubbornly as I looked over at him.

Over the past few weeks, Robert had tried his hardest to pay for a cell phone for me, but I'd refused. There was no way I'd let him add me to his plan. I'd even talked to him about his other gifts two weeks ago. While Sarah had been delighted every time a package showed up at my work, I hadn't appreciated them nearly as much. It just felt wrong to me. I understood he had been doing it because he wanted to take care of me, but it made me uncomfortable.

"I assume I'm taking you back to the diner?" he asked after a moment of silence.

"Yeah. My car is parked there." I looked away.

He'd also tried on several occasions to take me home. Over and over, I'd used the excuse that my car was at the diner. I could tell he was starting to get upset, but I still couldn't bring myself to tell him that I was living at the gym.

Other than a few brief arguments over his gifts and where I lived, the past few weeks had been wonderful. Robert was the kind of man who took time to be with and listen to his girlfriend. When I had a bad day, he would let me vent to him. He was always so attentive, like everything I said and did really mattered to him. I'd never been happier. It was nice to have someone who truly cared about me.

He stayed silent until we pulled up next to my car. "You promise you'll get a cell phone soon?"

I nodded.

"All right then."

"I love the fact that you worry about me, but you really don't have to," I said.

"I don't like not knowing where you are."

"I'm either at work or at home. Don't worry."

"That's another thing. Why won't you let me take you home, Claire? What are you hiding?"

Dread filled me. I didn't want to argue with him over this. "I'm not hiding anything. It's just easier for you to drop me off here."

"Why won't you even give me an address?" he asked.

"I'm ashamed of where I live, okay?" I finally said.

"Oh, Claire. We've talked about this. I know our financial situations are different, but you can't possibly think that I'd care about something like that. I want you to be mine. That's the truth. Whether you have ten dollars or ten thousand dollars is irrelevant."

I shrugged. "I should probably go. I have to work in the morning."

He sighed. "All right, I'll see you later. If I have time, I'll stop by the diner tomorrow night."

I leaned across the console and kissed him. "I'll see you then."

I climbed out of his car and unlocked mine. He waited until I was safely inside before pulling away. I ran my hands through my hair in aggravation. I couldn't keep lying to him like this. I needed to find an apartment, and I needed to find it quickly. I knew he was tired of me hiding things from him. Things had been going so good, and I didn't want to ruin them over something like this.

Robert had stuck to his word about taking it slow. He hadn't done anything besides kiss me yet. He was such a gentleman, nothing like the boys I'd gone out with in high school. I loved that he knew I needed time to ease into this, and he hadn't pressured me for more. If things kept going the way they had been, I would be willing to move to the next step soon.

I climbed out of my car a few minutes later and headed for the gym. Sam was sitting at the counter when I walked in. I stopped and talked to her for a few minutes before heading up to Bob's office. I unlocked the door and flicked on the lights.

After changing into a pair of shorts and a tank top, I dropped down onto the couch and covered myself with the thin blanket. Just as I was drifting off, I heard a knock on the door. Thinking it was someone looking for the restroom or something, I ignored it. After another minute or so, I heard a louder knock.

I sighed in defeat as I climbed off the couch, and I walked to the door. I peered through the small peephole in the door, trying to see who it was. My heart stopped when I saw Robert standing there.

No, this can't be happening.

I darted away from the door and pressed myself up against the wall, praying that he hadn't heard me.

He knocked again. "Claire, I know you're in there. Open the damn door!"

I closed my eyes in defeat. It was over. The jig was up. After taking one look at this room, he'd know that I was living here and that I was technically homeless. He'd never speak to me again.

I unlocked the door and slowly opened it. Robert pushed through before I had a chance to say anything. He took one look at my makeshift bed on the couch before turning to face me. He was angry. I could see it written all over his face.

"Why?" he asked.

"Why what?" I winced at the sound of my voice. It sounded so small, so defeated.

"Why didn't you tell me the truth? Jesus, Claire, we've been together for over a month. You didn't think to bring up the fact that you're living in a gym?"

"It's only temporary, I swear. I'm saving everything I can to get an apartment. You weren't supposed to find out—"

"Find out what? That you're homeless? This is bullshit, Claire. You should've told me. I would've helped you."

"I was ashamed, okay? I knew that if you found out and didn't leave me, you'd try to help me. I don't want help. I won't take handouts. I want to be able to say that I'm capable of taking care of myself!"

"Claire, I'm so tired of watching you struggle. This is the last straw!"

I froze. This was it. He was going to wash his hands of me and move on.

"What do you mean?" I asked, terrified to hear him say the words.

"I've left you alone and let you handle your own life. I can't do it anymore. I want you to pack your things. You're coming home with me," Robert said.

"Wait, what?" I asked.

"You heard me. Pack your things."

"I can't do that," I said, still not completely understanding what he was asking of me.

There was no way he had just asked me to move in with him.

"Why not?" he asked, annoyance clear in his voice.

"You really want me to move in with you?" I asked.

"Of course I do. I'm not leaving you here, Claire. Now, pack your things, or I'll do it for you."

"But I can't move in with you. We've only been together a few weeks," I said stupidly.

"I don't care. You're not living in a damn gym!"

He walked across the room and started gathering the few things I didn't have in my suitcase. I just stood there and watched him, my mind trying to process what was happening. I was torn between fighting him or just giving in. I was afraid that if I refused to go with him, he'd leave me permanently. As scared as I was of what lay ahead, I was also terrified of being without him. Even though we had only been together for a few weeks, he made me feel so good about myself.

Once everything was packed and I'd slipped on my shoes, he picked up my suitcase and turned back to me. "Come on, let's go."

I followed him down the stairs and out to his car in a daze. He threw my suitcase in the backseat as I climbed into the passenger seat. He climbed into the car and started the engine. We were both silent for a few minutes.

Finally, I found my voice. "I won't stay with you for long, I promise. I'll find a place of my own. I almost have enough money." I didn't want to be a burden on him. I could take care of myself. I always had before.

"Bullshit. You're not leaving, Claire. I'm tired of playing these damn games with you. You're moving in, and you're not leaving. Do you understand?"

I nodded. "Yes."

"Finally, she's reasonable!" Robert threw his hand in the air while still driving with the other.

"Thank you for doing this for me," I said.

"Of course. I told you, you're mine. I take care of what's mine."

"You've been so good to me," I whispered. "I don't know what I did to deserve your kindness."

He glanced over at me. "Claire, I know you haven't had the best life, but you need to accept help when people offer it to you. Pride will only get you so far."

"I know."

"How did you end up in the gym anyway?"

"My boss owns the gym, too. When he found out I was living in my car, he convinced me to move in there."

"You were living in your..." He took a deep breath. "Never mind. I'm not asking, or I'll just get pissed off again. How long have you been at the gym?"

"Since the night we met."

He growled under his breath, "Unbelievable, Claire. I don't even know what to say."

"I'm sorry I lied to you. I didn't want you to know."

"It doesn't matter now. Where are the rest of your things?"

I gave him a confused look. "What do you mean?"

"Your suitcase is in the backseat. Where are the rest of your belongings? Do you have them stored somewhere?"

"Oh! Um…no. I don't have anything else."

"You mean to tell me everything you own is in that suitcase?"

"Yeah."

"I'll take care of it," he said shortly.

"Take care of what?"

"Claire, you have *nothing*. I'll have clothes sent to the house for you."

"What? No! What I have is fine!"

"We're done talking about this."

He turned off the main road. He stopped in front of a gate and rolled his window down. I watched in amazement as he punched in a series of numbers into a box beside the car.

"The passcode is nine-two-four-six."

Once he finished hitting buttons, the gate opened slowly. Once we drove through, I turned to see the gate closing. I was in a different world now. I turned my attention back to where we were headed. A house came into view—no, not a house. It was a mansion. My mouth dropped open in amazement as I stared at it. Since it was dark, I couldn't see much of it. What I could see blew me away. The house was made of stone and two stories high. The front porch had two white pillars holding the roof up. On the second story, I could see where a set of doors opened up to a balcony.

"This is where you live?" I asked.

"Home sweet home." He parked in front of the house. As soon as he shut off the car, he was out of the vehicle and opening the back door to get my suitcase.

It took me longer to climb out. I was still in shock over the size of his home. *Dear God, what have I gotten myself into? Why does a man like this want me?*

Once I was finally out of the car, I followed Robert up the porch steps and to the front door. He unlocked it and stepped inside. After disabling the alarm, he turned on the lights. I stepped in behind him and stared. The foyer was just as breathtaking as the outside of the home. The floors were a dark wood. A statue of an angel was next to a set of stairs leading to the second floor. A few pieces of art were hanging on the walls, but I found it strange that there were no family photos.

"To the right is the kitchen and dining room. The living room is to the left. The first-floor bathroom is behind the staircase. The laundry room is also back there, but I have a maid, so you won't have to worry about going in there. The back door is over there, too. I have a swimming pool in the backyard, and you're welcome to use it."

I looked around. "Wow. I don't even know what to say. Your home is beautiful."

"It's your home now, too. What's mine is yours."

"I'll never be able to repay you for this," I said quietly as I looked down at the floor in front of me. My worn-out tennis shoes and sleep clothes looked ten times worse when I was standing in this house. I could never fit into a life like this.

"Just stay here, and keep me happy. That's all I ask." Robert stepped closer to me.

I relaxed as his hand cupped my face.

"I'm sorry for being so angry with you earlier. I should've handled it better."

"It's not your fault. I should've been honest with you."

He leaned down and brushed his lips against mine. The kiss grew deeper as he pulled me against him. When we finally pulled apart, his breathing was uneven.

"Now comes the hard part." Robert released me. "Would you like to stay in my room with me? Or would you prefer a room of your own?"

My eyes widened in shock. I hadn't even thought about where I'd be sleeping. "Oh, I don't—"

"If you're not comfortable staying with me, it's fine." He smiled.

"I think I'd rather have a room of my own, if that's okay with you."

"That's fine. You don't have to stay in mine"—he paused—"yet. I'll get you in there eventually."

I grinned at the wicked smile on his face.

"Come on. I'll show you to your new room."

I followed him up the steps. At the top, one hallway led in two different directions. He turned right. There were three doors along the hallway. He stopped in front of the closest one and swung the door open. After he switched on the lights, we stepped inside.

I stared at the room. It was ten times bigger than Bob's office. The room was bigger than most of the houses where I'd lived while in foster care. The walls were a pale pink color. The floor was hardwood, just like in the foyer. A dark king-sized bed with cream-colored bedding sat to the left. A dresser, matching the bed, sat directly across from it. A vanity stood a few feet away from the dresser with a mirror built into the top. There was a large desk with a flat screen computer monitor by the bed on my left. I took a few steps forward and opened a door on the right side of the room. After turning on the light, I saw a walk-in closet.

"It's incredible," I whispered as I walked back out of the closet.

"I thought you'd like it. This wing of the house has a bathroom right down the hall on the left. If you need me for something during the night, my room is on the opposite side of the house." Robert set my suitcase down on the bed. "Do you have to work tomorrow?"

"Yeah."

He nodded. "My maid, Ellie, will be here in the morning. I'll let her know you're staying with us now. When you go to work, take the black Audi in the garage. The keys are hanging by the front door. I'll write down the security codes for the house and gate, so you have them. I know you're going to fight me, but the Audi is yours now."

I opened my mouth to argue, but he held up a hand to stop me.

"No. You're driving it. Your car isn't safe, and no offense but my neighbors would probably have a heart attack if they saw your car pulling up to my house. They'd probably call the police. I have to be in court early tomorrow, but I'll stop on the way home and pick up a cell phone for you. Again, this isn't up for debate. You're staying with me now, Claire, and I'm going to handle things for you, so get used to it."

It took everything in me not to glare at him. I was angry that he had decided to take complete control of my life, but I couldn't really protest too much right now. I was living in his house, so I had to follow his rules. It was a lot like moving into a new foster home. Only this time, it was much nicer.

"At least let me pay rent or help you with the bills." I frowned at him.

"No. You're my guest, not my tenant. If you want, you can quit your job. That'll give you more free time. You could apply to WVU."

My mouth dropped open in shock. "Then, I'd be completely dependent on you!"

"Is that a problem for you?"

"Yes! Yes, it is! What happens if we split? I'll be worse off than I am now!" I said angrily.

He stepped closer to me. "Let me clear this up for you. We're not going to *split*. We're in this for the long haul. I know we haven't been together for very long, but you're mine now, Claire. I'm not letting you go, okay? You're too important to me to just give up. No matter what the future holds for us, we'll get through it. I'll make sure of it."

He sounded so confident that I couldn't help but believe him. He truly cared about me, and he was determined to keep us together.

My anger evaporated. "Okay," I whispered.

He leaned down and gently kissed me. "I'm off to bed, but I'll see you tomorrow evening. Do you work the day after tomorrow?"

I shook my head.

"Good. Don't plan anything. I have a surprise for you."

I smiled. "I can't wait."

He kissed me briefly before turning for the door.

Just as he was about to leave, I called out, "Robert?"

"Yes?" He turned back toward me.

"You said you have a son. When will I get to meet him? What should I say if I see him tomorrow before I leave for work?"

"Cooper isn't here. He's at the beach with one of his friends. He'll be back this weekend though. I'll warn you now, he's been a bit…hard to deal with since his mother died. He's built up a lot of anger from her death. When you meet him, don't be surprised if he's rude. You just have to overlook that."

"Oh, okay." My stomach sank.

I understood what Robert hadn't said. Cooper was going to hate me and make sure that I knew I wasn't welcome here.

Robert said, "Good night," before closing the bedroom door behind him.

Once he was gone, I opened my suitcase and pulled out my clothes and toiletries. I put the toiletries on the dresser before sorting through my clothes. I threw the dirty ones in the hamper next to the door. Then, I put my bras and underwear in one of the drawers in the dresser. My sleep clothes went in next and then my socks. Finally, I hung up my good clothes in the closet. They only took up a tiny portion of one wall. I stared at them, realizing just how little I really had. The knowledge that I really didn't belong in Robert's world began to creep in.

I turned away before I gave myself time to think about it anymore. I kicked off my shoes next to my bed and pulled the covers down. I sighed in bliss as I lay down on the bed. After spending weeks in my car and then on a couch, this bed felt like heaven. I snuggled further down into the covers, too exhausted to stay awake any longer.

When I awoke the next morning, it took me a few minutes to figure out where I was. Then, it all came back to me. I was living with Robert now. I rolled over and snuggled down into the covers as I tried to process the events of last night.

I was with Robert even though he'd found out that I had been living in the gym. He hadn't left me like I'd expected him to. Instead, he'd taken me in and promised to take care of me. Yesterday, I'd had nothing more than a couch to sleep on, a crappy car, and one suitcase to hold the few belongings I had. Today, I had a new room, a new car, and more hope than I'd had in a long time.

I hadn't liked the way Robert forced so many things on me at once, but after sleeping on it, I understood where he was coming from. He simply wanted to take care of me. He might have been a bit bossy about it, but he was only looking out for me.

When it was time to get up for work, I crawled out of bed and grabbed one of my uniforms from the closet. After collecting underwear and my toiletries, I stepped out into the hallway. I couldn't remember which door was the bathroom, so I tried the first one I came to. Lucky for me, it was the right one. I slipped inside the bathroom and quietly closed the door behind me. I grabbed a couple of towels off a shelf and set them next to the large walk-in shower. I stripped out of my clothes and threw them into the hamper before turning on the water.

I walked into the shower and put my personal items on the shelf. I turned away from the water, letting it pelt my back. It felt incredible, and I relaxed as steam rose around me.

After a few minutes, I finally started washing my hair. Once that was finished, I showered quickly and shut off the water. I toweled off and then threw my hair in a towel to dry. After dressing in the nicest jeans and shirt I had, I took my hair out of the towel and blow-dried it. Once loose waves were hanging down my back, I inspected myself in the mirror. I looked different. It took me a minute to realize why. I was content. Moving in with Robert had taken so much worry off my mind.

I hurried down the stairs to the front door. I found a sticky note on the wall next to where the keys were hanging. I grabbed both and headed into the kitchen. Along with the gate and house combinations, the note said the garage entrance was in a separate room just past the dining room. I glanced around the kitchen as I hurried through it. All the appliances were stainless steel. The floor and walls were pristine white. Entering the dining room, I noticed the hardwood floors. The walls were a light cream color. A large table that could hold ten or more people sat in the center of the room. I shook my head in amazement as I walked to the door. I made sure to set the house alarm before walking into the garage.

The garage was big enough to hold four cars, but only the Audi was inside. I walked over to it and climbed in. After I finally figured out how to raise the garage door, I backed out and headed down the driveway. The gate opened as soon as I stopped in front of it.

I could really get used to this.

The drive to work was uneventful, but as soon as I pulled into the diner parking lot, that changed. Junie was walking toward the building and stopped when she saw me. Her eyes widened in surprise when I climbed out of my new car.

"You've got to be shitting me. A new car?" she asked.

I walked over to her, suddenly uncomfortable. "Um…yeah. It came with the package."

"Package?"

"I moved in with Robert last night. He found out about the gym and refused to let me stay there anymore. He also gave me this car." I shifted nervously as I waited to see how she'd react.

She shook her head. "You're getting in deep with him, aren't you?"

"I guess so. Is that a bad thing?"

"No, it's just…I don't know. I'm sure I'm just being overprotective, but I worry about you being with him."

"I told you before that you shouldn't. Robert is a good man. All he's doing is taking care of me and helping me. I really care about him. I lo—" I clamped my mouth shut, shocked that I'd almost said the L-word.

Love? There was no way I loved Robert yet. It was too soon. *Isn't it?* Falling in love with him wouldn't be hard. As I thought about it, I realized that I might already be.

"I'm going to pretend that you didn't just say that. Come on, let's get the diner ready," Junie said as she started walking again.

I followed her inside, the L-word still bouncing around my brain.

When I arrived home that night, I was surprised to find a note on my bed. I picked it up and read it.

> CLAIRE,
>
> I HAD NEW CLOTHES DELIVERED TO THE HOUSE TODAY. ELLIE CHECKED THE SIZES OF YOUR CLOTHING IN THE CLOSET TO MAKE SURE EVERYTHING WOULD FIT. I HOPE YOU LIKE THEM.
>
> ROBERT

I closed my eyes, trying to process what the note said. I couldn't believe that he'd bought me new things. I opened my eyes and walked over to the dresser.

Unsure of what I would find, I pulled the first drawer open. It was completely full. My eyes widened in shock as I picked up the first thing my hands touched—a pair of silky underwear. I dug through the drawer, checking out each piece of lingerie. He'd purchased every kind of underwear out there—from boy shorts to pieces of string that could barely pass for underwear.

I closed the drawer and opened the next one. It was also full, but this time, it was bras. I picked up one and stared at it. When I saw the brand name, I dropped it back into the drawer. None of these were like the cheap ones I usually wore. No, they were expensive and sexy.

I bit my lip as I closed the drawer and hurried over to the walk-in closet. I threw the door open and flipped on the switch.

Oh my God.

Last night, the closet had been empty, except for a small corner where I'd hung my clothes. Now, it was full of dresses, jeans, shirts, shorts, jackets, dressy clothes I'd never wear, and shoes.

Oh, the shoes…

There were at least twenty pairs. Some were heels, some sandals, a few pairs of running shoes, and even a pair of Converse.

I closed the door and walked over to my bed. I dropped down onto it and picked up Robert's note. I had no clue what to think.

It's too much. I can't handle all this at once.

I knew Robert was only trying to help me, but his generosity was starting to worry me. I'd only been with him for a month, but I already felt overwhelmed. The money he had spent on me so far made it seem like we'd been together for years. I'd never been in a relationship before, but to me, it seemed like we were moving way too fast. First a room, then a car, and now clothes… I was starting to feel more than a little freaked out.

I knew what I had to do. When he came home tonight, I was going to sit down and talk to him. If I explained how I felt, maybe he would understand why he couldn't keep buying me things. I didn't want to throw his gifts back in his face, but I couldn't accept them either. They were just too much, too fast.

Decision made, I stood and walked to the dresser. I dug through the clothes until I found a pair of yoga pants and a tank top that I'd brought with me. After changing into them, I threw my work uniform into the hamper. I frowned when I realized the clothes I'd put in there last night were gone. Obviously, Robert's maid had washed my clothes for me. Maybe I was being stupid, but I didn't want her to wash my clothes. I was staying here rent-free, so the least I could do was wash my own laundry.

Forcing my annoyance aside, I lay down on the bed and grabbed my e-reader off the nightstand. I needed a distraction until Robert came home. Reading would keep my mind off of everything going on in my life.

Three hours later, I heard a knock on my bedroom door. I yelled for Robert to come in as I put my e-reader down on the nightstand.

He opened the door and walked in. The smile on his face was infectious. I grinned back as he sat down on the bed.

"I could most certainly get used to this." He leaned over and kissed me.

"Get used to what?" I asked when he pulled away.

"Coming home every night and seeing you in my house." He reached into his pocket and pulled out a phone. "This is for you."

My happiness over the kiss disappeared as I took the phone from him. It was a smartphone. I'd seen television ads for them, so I knew they weren't cheap.

"I told you that I didn't need a phone." I put the phone down.

"And I told you I wasn't arguing with you over it."

I sat up. "I think we need to talk, Robert."

He gave me a questioning look. "Okay…"

"Look, I really appreciate everything you've done for me. No one has ever cared enough about me to do the things you've done. But I can't keep accepting gifts from you. The car, the clothes, the phone—they're all too much. I know you're trying to take care of me, but it's just too much at once. It makes me feel uncomfortable."

"Why would you feel uncomfortable? Most women love when men buy them presents." He frowned at me.

"I'm not most women. I don't want you to think I'm only using you for your money, and that's what it looks like. I just feel like we're moving too fast."

Anger flashed in his eyes, shocking me.

"I know you're not using me. You've fought me tooth and nail on every single thing I've given you. No, you're not like other women. You're innocent and kind. That's why I'm with you and not with someone else. I'm sorry that the gifts bother you, but I'm not going to stop buying things for you."

"Robert—" I started.

He cut me off as he said, "No, we're done talking about this. You're mine, and I plan to make sure that you're taken care of. You will never want for anything again. All I ask for in exchange is that you stay with me. I love you, Claire. I have since the moment I laid eyes on you."

My mouth dropped open in shock. *He loves me?* "You can't love me, Robert. You don't even know me that well."

"Yes, I do. You think that I'd let a stranger stay in my house? I've done a lot of research on you, Claire. I know about every single foster home you lived in. I've read your records. Time and time again, CPS noted how you took care of the other kids and how caring you were." He took a deep breath. "And I know about Jason."

My entire body froze. *No, he can't know.* "I don't know what you're talking about."

"Bullshit. I know what he did to you. I saw the pictures. He nearly beat you to death, Claire."

Jason was one of my foster siblings. It had been so long since I even thought about him. When I was fourteen, I'd moved in with the Jones family, and he had been the only other foster kid. He was two years older than me, and we'd become friends almost instantly. For months, he had been my best friend. He'd even protected me at school when some of the other kids made fun of me for being in foster care.

One night, he'd come home drunk. Our foster parents had already been asleep, so I'd unlocked the door to let him in. He had been so drunk that he could barely walk. I'd somehow managed to get him to his room without waking anyone up. When I'd helped him lie down on the bed, he'd pulled me down with him. At first, I'd thought it was because he was so drunk. Then, he'd started whispering dirty things in my ear as he tried to pull my tank top off. I'd kicked him to get away, but that had only made him angry. He'd called me a whore and a tease as he beat me. By the time our foster parents had woken up, I'd passed out.

The weeks following that night had been horrible. I'd been ripped out of the home and placed with another foster family. Jason had been arrested for assault and battery. The cops had pressed charges against him, and I had been pretty much forced to testify against him by the police and my new foster parents. He'd been convicted as an adult, and as far as I knew, he was still in jail.

After that night, I'd closed myself off from my foster siblings. It wasn't until I'd met Shelly that I let myself trust again. The little girl had wormed her way into my heart in a matter of weeks. No one had managed to do that in years.

"You had no right to look into my past," I said as tears filled my eyes.

"I wanted to know more about you, Claire, and you refused to talk about the past."

"Because I didn't want you to know!" I shouted.

I wasn't sure if I was crying from the pain of the memories or because I was so angry with Robert. It was probably both. He'd invaded my privacy, and he made me remember things that I'd buried long ago.

"You can't hide things from me. What's in the past doesn't matter. You're so broken, Claire, and you don't even realize it."

"I want to be alone." I looked away from him.

"Claire, talk to me," Robert said.

I shook my head. "Just go. Please."

He sighed, and I felt the bed shift when he stood up.

"All right, I'll give you some time. I won't apologize for searching into your past though, Claire. I had a right to know."

I didn't say a word. I couldn't. I was too angry at the moment, and I knew I'd say something that I might regret later.

"Don't forget that I have a surprise planned for you tomorrow. A car will pick you up at nine in the morning."

When the door closed, I started sobbing. I was so hurt and angry over what he'd done. He'd investigated me, like I was one of his cases that he would talk about. I felt violated. My past was mine, and he had no right to search into it. He should've respected me enough not to pry.

I scooted down the bed and lay down again. After a while, my tears finally dried, and all I had left was anger. No matter what I said, Robert wouldn't listen to me. He'd still continue to buy me things even after I explained to him why I didn't want them. He'd continue to search for answers when I didn't want to give them. Whatever I said wouldn't matter.

I closed my eyes and threw my arm over my face. He'd said he loved me. But how could he? If he did, he wouldn't have dug into my past like that. For the first time since I'd met Robert, I wasn't sure if I wanted anything to do with him. Finally, sleep took me, but my dreams were troubled the entire night.

When I awoke the next morning, my head was throbbing. After digging through my purse for a bottle of headache medicine, I took a few pills, hoping that they would help. I opened the dresser and grabbed underwear before heading to the bathroom to shower.

I felt horrible. The anger from the night before had drained me of energy. The fact that I'd had trouble sleeping probably wasn't helping either. I showered quickly, dried off, and pulled on my underwear.

I remembered that Robert had said a car would be picking me up at nine. Glancing at the clock on the bathroom wall, I saw that I only had half an hour to get ready. I debated on staying home since I was so mad at him. The pure rage I'd felt last night was gone, but I was still angry.

I was quickly learning that Robert was all about control. He hadn't been intentionally cruel to me, but the fact that he was now in control of almost every part of my life bothered me.

In the end, I decided to go. If I stayed home all day, I would only mope about what had happened last night. I tried to look at things from his side. In his own way, he had only been trying to help me and get to know me better.

I didn't approve of how he'd handled everything though. Total and complete trust wouldn't happen overnight, especially from me. If he'd given me time to get to know him better, I probably would've told him about my past and all the ugly things I'd endured.

I pushed my troubled thoughts away as I scrambled to get ready. I didn't bother with makeup since I was running late. I braided my hair while it was still wet. Not the best way to show up for a surprise, but I didn't have much of a choice.

I dressed quickly before running downstairs and out the front door to where a car was waiting on me. I hurried to the black Cadillac SUV and climbed inside.

As soon as I closed the door, the car took off. Now that I was no longer rushing to get ready, my thoughts from earlier came back. I sighed as I realized that Robert and I were truly in a relationship now. We'd even had our first fight. I had no doubt that relationships were hard and ours would be no different. I needed to let go of the anger I felt toward him and move on.

By the time the driver took me to my destination, I'd decided to let it go. I would still talk to him and explain why his prying had made me so angry, but I wasn't going to hold a grudge. There was no point.

It turned out that my surprise was a spa. After Robert's driver promised that he would be waiting for me when I was finished, I walked inside and nervously looked around. I'd never been to a spa before, and I had no clue what to expect.

A woman in her mid-thirties sat behind a reception desk, and I walked over to her.

As soon as she saw me, she smiled. "Hi, can I help you?"

"Um…yeah, I have an appointment here—or at least, I think I do."

She gave me a strange look. "Okay. What is the name on the reservation?"

I gave her Robert's name. The moment it left my lips, her eyes widened in shock.

"Of course. Come with me."

I followed her across the room and down a hallway. She opened a door and motioned me inside. I walked in and looked around. A table stood in the middle of the floor. Several potted plants were in the room, and soothing music played from hidden speakers.

"Mr. Evans arranged for you to have the full package today," the receptionist said.

"The full package? What does that include?" I asked.

"A facial, Swedish massage, a pedicure and manicure, and a bikini wax."

My mind skipped over everything else and landed on the wax part. "Whoa, wait a minute. A bikini wax?"

She nodded. "Yes, we'll also wax your eyebrows and legs for you. Mr. Evans also instructed us to style your hair."

"I've never had any part of me waxed before," I said nervously. I didn't usually handle pain well.

"Don't worry. Everyone hears horror stories about how painful bikini waxes are, but I assure you that they're not that bad," she said.

She lied.

Twenty minutes later, I was biting my lip so hard that I could taste blood as I tried not to scream. The bikini wax was the most embarrassing and painful experience of my life. Having my legs and eyebrows waxed hadn't been much better. When we finished, I limped to the next room for my massage, cursing Robert and the woman who had waxed my lady bits.

The massage went much better. I enjoyed it so much that I *almost* forgave Robert for scheduling the waxing. The facial came next. I had to admit that being pampered was something I could get used to.

The spa staff brought me fruity drinks while I was getting my manicure and pedicure. By my third one, I realized that they had alcohol in them even though I couldn't taste it. I'd never had alcohol in my life, and the drinks were hitting me hard. The world grew fuzzy as I watched a woman paint my toenails.

I still felt strange when they sent me to the salon a few doors down from the nail place. The stylist gave me a strange look as I practically fell down into the chair, but she didn't comment on my behavior.

"What are we doing with your hair?" she asked.

I stared at my reflection in the mirror as she took out my braid, debating on what to do. My hair had always been the same—long and one length. I wasn't sure if I wanted to change it.

"Can you just trim it and maybe add a few layers?" I asked.

"Sure. Your hair is gorgeous. I understand why you want to keep it long."

I watched as she pinned part of my hair up, and then she started cutting. She trimmed just enough to get rid of my split ends. When she finished, she gave me a mirror so that I could see what she'd done. I'd always trimmed my own hair, so I smiled when I saw how much prettier it looked, and I realized that cosmetology school wasn't in the cards for me.

"Thank you. It looks so much better!"

"You're very welcome. It's amazing what some layers can do. Now, let's get your makeup done."

She pulled a cart over to me. It was covered with makeup and some things I didn't recognize. Besides foundation, eyeliner, and eye shadow, I didn't really mess with makeup much. As she worked, she took the time to explain how to apply everything. When she finished, all I could do was stare into the mirror in shock. I looked the same but completely different.

"Thank you," I gushed.

"I'm glad to help. You're a beautiful girl, and with the right amount of makeup, you are a total stunner," she said to me. "I'm supposed to give you a package, too. I'll be right back."

I continued to stare at my reflection as she left the room. When she returned a few minutes later, she was carrying a package similar to the one Robert had sent my dress in so long ago.

She handed it to me, and I opened it carefully. My breath caught as I stared at another dress and a pair of heels. Both were absolutely gorgeous. I picked the dress up out of the box and stared at it. The color was a deep red, matching the lipstick I was now wearing and the shoes still in the box. It was strapless with a flowing skirt that would just touch my knees when I put it on.

"You're supposed to change into that before you leave here," she instructed, pointing to a door marked *Dressing Room.*

"Why?" I asked, confused.

She shrugged. "No clue."

With the package, I walked to the dressing room and closed the door behind me. I stripped out of my clothes, careful not to mess up my makeup as I pulled my shirt over my head. I put my clothes into the box the dress had come in before carefully pulling on the dress and then the heels.

I turned in front of the mirror, checking out the dress. It had a hint of edginess to it while still looking classy and sophisticated. I loved it. I walked back out into the salon with the box tucked under my arm.

The hairstylist smiled at me. "You look wonderful. We're finished with you. A car is parked outside, waiting on you."

I profusely thanked her before heading toward the exit. Sure enough, Robert's driver was waiting for me. He helped me into the car before closing the door behind me.

The driver climbed behind the wheel of the SUV. "I'm supposed to drop you off at Mr. Evans's office."

"Oh…okay," I said, surprised.

Robert had never once invited me to his office. I didn't even know where it was.

We drove across town in silence. When we reached the middle of the city, the car turned down a side street. A few minutes later, we stopped in front of a two-story brick building with *Law Office of Robert Evans* written across the top of it. I thanked the driver before climbing out of the SUV and walking into the building.

The reception area was gorgeous. The walls were a light cream color with artwork hanging every few feet. There were two leather couches with a television mounted on the wall across from them. A glass table covered in magazines sat in the middle of the room.

A receptionist greeted me with a smile when I approached her desk.

"Hi, I'm here to see Robert," I said.

"What's your name?" she asked.

"Claire."

"Great. Have a seat, and I'll let him know you're here." She picked up her phone.

I walked across the room and sat down on one of the couches. I heard her speak into the phone briefly before hanging up.

"Claire, he's ready to see you." She pointed to a hallway across from her. "Go clear to the end of the hallway, and his door is on the right."

I followed her instructions and knocked on Robert's door. A second later, the door swung open. He opened his mouth to greet me, but then he stopped dead when he took in my appearance.

"Hi," I said, suddenly feeling self-conscious.

"Claire, you look amazing." He took my hand and led me into his office. He closed the door behind us.

"Thank you," I said as I looked around his office.

It looked similar to the reception area. A leather couch sat in the corner, and art was hanging on every wall. His desk was a dark mahogany color. Two plush chairs sat in front of it.

I took a seat in one of them.

He sat down in his chair, directly across from me. "Did you enjoy your surprise?"

"I did. Thank you, Robert. I wanted to apologize for last night. I shouldn't have been so angry with you. I don't approve of what you did, but I understand why you did it."

"I didn't think you would get so angry over it. If I had known, I would've tried harder to get you to talk to me."

"I know. It's just that my past isn't pretty, and I'd rather not think about it."

"I understand, but I hope you can see my side, too. I'm going to be blunt. I have a lot of power in this town. The press also watches me constantly. I knew that I wanted you to be a permanent fixture in my life, and I had to make sure that you weren't hiding anything. If you were and the press found out about it, I would be the one who suffered."

"Why would I matter to the press?" I asked, confused about where he was going with this.

"Because once I make our relationship public, things will change. There will be a lot of speculation about you just because of our age difference. Add in the fact that I lost my wife a year ago, and the rumors will run rampant. I don't want you or my reputation to be hurt. I had to be sure that you were who you said you were."

I'd never even thought of that. To me, Robert was just my boyfriend, but to everyone else, he was a powerful attorney. Even I'd seen the many articles about him that day in the library.

"I don't even know what to say. I'm so sorry," I said.

"Don't be upset, Claire. You had no clue what you were walking into." He hesitated. "While we're on the subject, I'd like to discuss something else with you."

"What?" I asked.

"I know we haven't been together that long, but I can't help from loving you. When I look at you, all I see is the future. I want you to be mine in every way, Claire."

I was shocked. This was the second time he'd told me that he loved me. I knew I cared deeply for Robert, but I wasn't entirely sure if I truly loved him yet. It was definitely a possibility, but I'd never loved someone before, not really, and I'd never had someone love me, so the emotion was foreign to me.

"I don't know what to say," I finally said.

"I know it seems like we're moving fast, but time isn't important to me. When I want something, I take it. Claire, I want you."

"I'm yours, Robert. I've told you that already."

"I know you have, but I want something…more." He stood and walked around the desk.

I looked up at him when he stopped beside me.

"More?" I asked, completely confused by his statement.

He took a deep breath as he pulled something out of his pocket. My heart stopped when I saw him holding a jewelry box.

No…he wouldn't.

"I want you to be my wife." He opened the box and revealed an engagement ring. "Will you marry me, Claire?"

Several moments passed in silence. Unable to find my voice, all I could do was shake my head. He stared at me, his eyes pleading with me to say something, anything.

"I know this is unexpected—" he said quietly.

"You think?" I blurted out, unable to stop myself.

"I want you to be my wife, Claire. The way I feel about you…it's like my entire world is driven by those emotions. We don't need to have a big wedding, if that's what you're worried about. We can go to the courthouse or have someone come to the house."

"I…you…" I started but stopped. I took a deep breath to collect my thoughts. "Robert, marriage is a big deal. It's not something that I take lightly."

"Of course it's a big deal! I've thought this over a million times, trying to talk myself out of asking you so soon, but I can't help the way I feel. Please marry me, Claire. You'll never want for anything as long as I'm around. Everything you've ever dreamed of having is within your grasp. All you have to do is say yes."

"I'm not ready to get married yet. I'm only eighteen! I have so many things I want to do before I settle down."

"You can still do them, Claire. Marrying me wouldn't mean that you'd be giving up your own life. You can do anything and go anywhere. All you have to do is ask. I would never deny you anything."

I stared up at him, unable, or maybe unwilling, to process what he was saying. All I could think of was the foster homes I'd lived in. Most of them had included married couples. Almost all of those had been unhappily married couples. The fighting, the yelling, the threats all rang in my ears as if I were witnessing them all over again. To me, marriage was a trap people were pulled into, full of promises of happiness when it actually led to nothing more than anger and sadness.

"Robert, I don't know. I've never even thought about getting married. Almost all my foster parents were miserable *because* they were married. The things I saw growing up kept me from ever wishing that on myself."

He crouched down next to me with a sad smile on his face. "Some marriages don't work out, but some do. I was married for a long time, and I can promise you that I was happy with Marie. Yes, we argued from time to time, but that happens no matter how strong a marriage is. Overall, we were happy though. If you give me a chance, I'll show you just how happy you can be. Please, Claire, please say you'll marry me."

"I-I need to think on this, okay? I'm not telling you no, but I'm not saying yes either."

"That's fine. I can wait a few days for you to decide." He stood, pulling me up with him. "I love you so much, Claire. I swear, you won't regret this if you say yes."

Before I could reply, he pulled me to him and kissed me deeply. Content, I relaxed my body into his. As his lips explored mine, I willed myself to feel the spark I so desperately craved from his kisses. I pulled away, feeling defeated.

"I think I want to go home now," I said quietly.

"Of course. I'll have my driver, Frank, take you home," Robert said before gently kissing my forehead. "We can have dinner at home tonight instead of going out like I had planned."

"I can't wait," I murmured as I headed for the door.

With one final glance behind me, I walked out of the office. I kept my eyes glued to the floor until I was out of the building.

The ride back to the house was completely silent. I stared out the window as I tried to process what had just happened in Robert's office. I knew that he cared about me—he wouldn't have convinced me to move in with him if he didn't—but I'd never expected him to ask me to marry him.

Living in his house had been a big step, but compared to marriage, it was nothing. I'd never really thought about marriage. If I were being honest with myself, I'd never really thought about being in a serious relationship before Robert had invaded my life. I'd spent my entire life depending on no one but myself. I still wasn't used to having Robert take care of me. It wasn't that I didn't trust him. I just couldn't help but wait for something to rip us apart because that was how my life had been.

When I was younger, I would get attached to my foster parents. Some of them were truly kind, but most had only taken me in because a nice little check came with me. After being tossed from home to home, I'd finally realized that I couldn't let myself care about any of them. It had been too painful when I had to start over.

I'd carried that broken mentality around with me my entire life. Giving up the mindset now was proving to be much harder than I'd expected. I wanted to jump into things without thinking, but I couldn't. I had to be strong. I had to protect myself.

I knew marrying Robert would change everything for me. I'd never want for anything again. A weaker woman would have caved the moment he asked her to be his wife. The possibilities with him were endless. He had everything a woman desired—power, confidence, wealth, and kindness.

I let myself think about how my life could be if I did agree to marry him. I cared for Robert. I couldn't deny that. Over time, I knew I could grow to truly love him. If I told him no, he might force me out of his life. I didn't want that. The thought of continuing the way I was before I'd met him was almost unbearable. I'd been so alone, so broken.

As we pulled up to the house, I realized that I knew what my answer would be.

I would marry Robert even if I weren't in love with him. I would do it because I was weak, because I wanted him to take care of me.

With that realization, I felt like a cheap whore.

Since I still had several hours before Robert would come home, I decided to explore the house. I started with the kitchen and then continued walking around the first floor. I'd seen all of those rooms, so I headed upstairs. I turned down Robert's hallway, but I didn't go into his bedroom. I was sure he wouldn't mind, but I didn't want to pry, and I wasn't comfortable with looking in his room without his knowledge.

The only other room in his wing of the house was a bathroom. It was twice the size of mine. I shook my head as I closed the door and headed back toward my wing of the house. I was really out of my league.

Once I married him, all of this would be mine as well. It still didn't seem real. Things like this didn't happen in real life. At least, they didn't happen to people like me. A poor foster kid didn't normally end up marrying the rich lawyer. I couldn't help but wonder what the catch was. Life was being too kind to me right now. Surely, something bad would happen soon. The earth might open up and swallow me whole. Robert would probably end up kicking me out once he came to his senses. *Something* was going to go wrong for me. It always did.

There were two other doors in my wing besides my room and the bathroom. I tried the first door, but it was locked, so I moved on to the next. It was another guest bedroom, which made me think the locked door was Cooper's bedroom.

Curiosity got the better of me as I walked back to his door and tried it again. It was obviously still locked. I frowned as I couldn't help but wonder why Cooper's bedroom was locked. In every single foster home I'd been in, the children's rooms were never allowed to be locked.

I shrugged and headed back to my room. I closed the door behind me before lying down on my bed. I still wasn't used to the silence that seemed to be the norm in this house. At almost all my foster homes, I had lived with other kids, and they were always noisy, especially the younger ones. Silence was a luxury that I wasn't used to.

I closed my eyes, taking in the tranquility of the moment. Before I knew it, I drifted off to sleep.

I awoke to the sound of someone knocking on my door. I glanced at the clock on my nightstand to see that it was already eight o'clock in the evening. I'd slept much longer than I expected.

I stood and walked to the door. When I opened it, I saw Robert standing on the other side. He gave me a small smile.

"Claire, I was hoping you would join me downstairs for dinner."

"Yes, of course." I yawned.

I stepped out of my room and followed him down the hall. When we reached the staircase, he took my hand in his.

"I thought we could grill outside," he said.

I smiled. "That sounds nice."

We stopped by the kitchen first where Robert grabbed a pack of premade hamburger patties and condiments out of the fridge and a pack of hamburger buns out of the cabinet. Before continuing outside, he pointed me in the direction of some plates, so I grabbed them and then followed him out the door. I stopped short as I took in his backyard for the first time. He'd mentioned that there was a pool, but he'd failed to tell me about the Jacuzzi and basketball court.

"Wow," I muttered under my breath as I looked around.

My eyes found their way back to the massive pool. It was near dusk now, and I could see the lights inside the pool.

I pulled my gaze away and followed Robert over to where the grill sat at the edge of the patio. I took the condiments and buns from him and put them down on a table a few feet away. Robert busied himself with throwing the hamburgers on the grill. I sat down in a nearby lounge chair and watched him as he worked. He'd changed out of his business suit and was now wearing a pair of khaki shorts and a polo shirt. Showing just how fit he was, the shirt hugged his chest and stomach, and his arms stretched the sleeves. I marveled at the fact that he was forty-two and in better shape than most guys in their twenties.

I also noticed that his hair was starting to gray just a bit around his temples. It wasn't much, but it was a reminder of our age difference. Robert, the man who wanted to marry me, was old enough to be my father. I shook my head, forcing those thoughts away. Age didn't matter. He'd said so himself over and over.

When the burgers were ready, he carried the plate to the table and set it down. I stood and walked over to the table. He smiled as he pulled me against him and kissed me. When he released me, we both sat down and started making our burgers. We ate in silence for a few minutes.

"How was the rest of your afternoon?" I asked.

"Good. I finished up a case that I've been working on for weeks. My client walked away with a nice settlement."

"That's great," I said as I finished off my hamburger.

"Don't talk with your mouth full, Claire. It isn't polite," he snapped.

Caught off guard by his sharp tone, all I could do was stare at him. Finally, I looked away. "Sorry."

He nodded. "I'm taking next week off now that the case is finished."

"How come?" I asked.

"To spend time with you. I know my schedule can be hectic at times. I hate that we have to work around it."

I shrugged. "It's your job. You can't help that you have crazy hours."

"I don't want you to think that I'm not spending enough time with you. I'm hoping that you'll reconsider my proposal after we spend some more time alone with each other," he said softly.

I looked up to see him watching me. The hope in his eyes prompted me to speak. "You really love me, don't you?"

He nodded. "I do. The way I feel about you is more than I ever felt for Marie. I feel like a dirty bastard for even saying that about her, but it's true. You're so pure, Claire. I can't help but love you."

I reached up and cupped his face. I ran my thumb over his bottom lip as I stared into his eyes. The vulnerability I saw in them tugged at my heart. Robert loved me. He would protect me and give me anything I asked for. The only thing he wanted in exchange was my heart. I knew I could give it to him. He wouldn't hurt me. I felt that deep in my bones.

"What happens if I tell you no, Robert?" I asked quietly. "Will you let me go?"

"I don't think I could handle being with you, knowing that you're unwilling to be my wife. I would feel as if you were simply using me," he said, his eyes never leaving mine.

I dropped my hand and looked away. "I would never use you, but I understand why you might think that."

Neither of us spoke for a minute.

Finally, I turned back to him. "If you truly love me, yes, I'll marry you."

When his eyes lit up with joy, I knew I'd made the right decision.

"God, Claire. Yes, I love you."

He pulled me to him and kissed me deeply. When we broke apart, he took the ring he'd shown me earlier out of his pocket. He held it up, so I could see it.

"After you left my office today, I decided that I would carry it with me always—just in case you said yes." He took my hand in his and slid the ring onto my finger.

"It's beautiful," I whispered as I stared at it.

It was white gold with a round diamond framed in additional diamonds. The band of the ring was also adorned in even more diamonds. I didn't even want to think about how much it had cost Robert.

"Just like you are." He leaned forward and kissed me again. "I'll make all the arrangements tomorrow. I know you don't want a big wedding, so I'll arrange for us to get married at the courthouse. It'll be quicker and easier this way. We'll be married by the end of next week."

I bit my lip to keep from saying anything. I'd never said I didn't want a wedding. He'd been the one to mention it earlier in his office. Truthfully, I would rather have a wedding. It would give me more time to prepare myself. The fact that he was planning on us being married next week terrified me. I'd expected more time.

"Great," I said weakly.

"Since I'm off next week, we'll go somewhere and spend a few days alone together," he said.

"Um…I still have to work, Robert. I wasn't expecting this to happen so soon."

"Don't be ridiculous. You have no need for that job now. You can quit."

"I like working there. Besides, what will I do all day if I don't have a job?" I asked.

"You can do whatever you want. Just call in tomorrow and let them know you're not coming back."

I shook my head. "I'm not quitting."

He frowned. "Don't be unreasonable, Claire. I refuse to let my wife work as a *waitress.*"

My temper flared. "What's wrong with being a waitress?"

"Nothing, Claire, but it's ridiculous that you want to continue working there. There's no point!"

"I'm not quitting, Robert," I said stubbornly.

He'd had a say over everything in my life so far, but I wouldn't give up my job. I loved my boss and the girls I worked with. I wouldn't just leave them. Besides, I wasn't the type to stay home and be the perfect little housewife. He would just have to deal with me being a *waitress.*

He sighed. "We'll discuss this more tomorrow. I have to go take care of a few things at work, but I'll be home by lunch. We can talk then."

"I won't be here," I said, trying not to show just how angry I was with him.

"Why not?"

"I'll be working."

His nostrils flared in irritation, but he wisely said nothing. I watched as he rose from his chair.

"I'm going to bed."

"Good night," I mumbled as I stared out across the yard.

If he'd bothered to reply, I didn't hear him.

I stayed in my chair for a long time once Robert was out of sight. I couldn't understand how he could go from kind and caring one minute to bossy and controlling the next. When he spoke, he would expect me to do whatever he told me, but that wasn't me.

A tiny voice in the back of my mind whispered that maybe I didn't really know him as well as I thought I did. Doubt flooded me until I felt like I was drowning.

I've already told him yes. I can't back out now.

I couldn't. It would ruin everything. He'd even told me that he wasn't sure he'd be able to stay with me if I refused to marry him. It almost felt like a trap.

I stood and walked over to the pool. I sat down on the edge of the shallow side and stuck my legs into the water. It was warmer than I'd expected. Even though it was still summer, the pool must be heated. I stared at one of the lights buried in the pool, watching the water ripple in its light. Suddenly, I wanted nothing more than to jump in. I bit my lip, debating on whether or not to do just that.

I looked around the yard. If I did jump in, I'd have to take off my dress. A high privacy fence surrounded the area, so no one would see me unless Robert came down to check on me. I doubted that he would since he'd told me that he was going to bed.

Decision made, I stood up and reached back to the zipper of my dress. I unzipped it and let it drop from my body. I felt naked, standing outside in only my bra and a thong that Robert had purchased for me. Both were far sexier than anything I'd ever owned before.

I stared down into the water. Feeling risqué, I let go of my inhibitions for the first time, and I made my choice. I took a deep breath, plugged my nose, and dived in. I stayed underwater for a few seconds, enjoying the absolute silence, before kicking my way to the surface. I laughed even though I wasn't sure why.

I swam across the pool, taking my time as I went. The warm water felt like liquid silk against my skin. Once I reached the edge of the pool, I dived under again. My stomach skimmed the bottom of the pool as I swam. When I couldn't hold my breath any longer, I broke the surface again.

One of my foster parents had taught me how to swim when I was younger, but it had been so long since I was in the water. I found it calming, which was just what I'd needed at the moment.

I continued swimming until my arms were aching from exertion. Finally, I swam to the steps and climbed out. I smiled, content from my swim, as I walked over to where I'd left my dress. I picked it up and headed for the house.

A cool breeze caused goose bumps to rise across my body, and my nipples hardened against the fabric of my skimpy bra. When I was about ten feet from the door, a different sensation hit my body. The hairs on the back of my neck stood up.

I looked around the yard, feeling like I was being watched. "Is anyone there?"

With the exception of the patio and the pool, Robert's entire yard was encased in shadows. A large elm tree sat several feet away from me, so that side of the patio was darker than the rest of the yard.

When I'd called out, I hadn't expected someone to actually answer me. I froze as a soft chuckle came from the shadows of the elm. A man stepped forward, and my entire body locked up in fear because it wasn't Robert.

"I have to say, if this is how I'm greeted every time I come home, I'm going to start hanging around more often," the man said as his eyes traveled down my body.

He stepped closer, and I automatically took a step back. He stopped once he was out of the shadows, allowing me to get my first good glance at him. He was tall, probably around six foot two, and he was built like a football player. The tight wifebeater he had on put his arm muscles as well as the hard planes of his chest and stomach on full display. I noted the dark tattoos covering his arms from shoulder to elbow on both sides.

His hair was a dark brown, so dark that it looked almost black, and his lips were full. But it was his eyes that stood out. They were the brightest emerald green I'd ever seen. Something in his eyebrow caught the light and glittered. My eyes widened when I realized that it was a looped piercing. That, along with his tattoos, screamed bad boy to me.

I was embarrassed as I realized that I'd been checking him out. I couldn't seem to help myself though. I finally understood the term *sex on a stick.*

"Who are you?" I finally asked once I managed to pry my eyes away from his body.

"The better question is, who are you? And why are you swimming around, almost naked, in my pool at ten o'clock at night? Don't get me wrong. I'm not complaining. I'm just curious as to who you are," he said, his eyes dropping to my chest.

My nipples tightened further, and I knew he could see them through my wet bra. My cheeks flamed in embarrassment until I realized what he'd said.

His pool?

"This isn't your pool. It's Robert's. And I happen to live here," I said.

His eyes were too busy leaving a trail of fire up and down my body to notice the angry glare I was giving him.

"Really? Well, isn't that convenient? Wanna share a room?"

"Who are you?" I demanded.

His eyes finally found mine again. "I'm Cooper—you know, Robert's son. I'm sure he's mentioned me before. Then again, maybe he hasn't. I doubt that he'd want a hot young girl like you to know that he has a twenty-year-old son. I bet I'm older than you are." He studied me for a minute. "If I didn't know my dad better, I would guess, from looking at you, that you're sixteen or seventeen. But even he's not that stupid. I'm going to say you're…eighteen. Am I right?"

I stared at him in shock. *This is Cooper? How is that even possible?* "You can't be Cooper."

"Why can't I?" he asked mockingly.

"Cooper is just a kid," I whispered.

Now that I was truly looking at him, I knew he was telling the truth. I could see some of Robert's features in him—the nose, the shape of his face, and other small characteristics that I had missed the first time.

He laughed. "Is that what he told you?"

I opened my mouth to say yes, but I stopped myself. Robert had never told me Cooper's age. I had just assumed that he was a child.

"No, I just thought…" I trailed off.

"I get it. It's hard to believe that your *boyfriend* has a kid who's older than you." He grinned wickedly. "At least, I assume he's your boyfriend since you're living here. You might just be his whore of the week though. I have to say, Dad has good taste."

"I'm not a whore!" I clutched my dress to my chest even though the gesture was pointless since he'd seen my body already.

He laughed, but it was humorless. His eyes lost their humor and turned cold. "I beg to differ. If you're fucking my dad, then yeah, you're a whore. That's the only type of women he messes with anymore."

My cheeks burned as anger flooded my body. "You know *nothing* about me, asshole!"

He stepped closer until he was right in front of me. "And I don't want to. I've seen your kind before."

I slapped him. I didn't even realize what I'd done until it was over. I covered my mouth in shock as we stared at each other.

"What the hell is going on out here?" a voice demanded.

I looked over as Robert came storming out of the house. He took one look at me before turning his attention to Cooper.

"What did you say to her?" Robert demanded.

Cooper shrugged. "Not a thing. I was just welcoming her to our home."

"Bullshit, Cooper. I saw her slap you."

"I didn't do anything." Cooper grinned at me. "Anyway, it was nice meeting you…"

"Claire. My name is Claire," I said through clenched teeth.

He hadn't even known my name, yet he'd assumed I was a whore. I decided then and there that Cooper was nothing more than an asshole.

I'd had so many plans when it came to him, but I had pictured a boy, not a man. I'd wanted to comfort him and let him know that I wasn't trying to take his mom's place. Those plans were now gone. Cooper didn't need comforting. He needed a swift kick in the junk.

"Good night, *Claire*," Cooper said before turning his attention to his dad. "As always, it's great to be home."

Robert and I watched in silence as Cooper disappeared into the house.

When he was gone, Robert turned to me. "What did he say to you, Claire?"

I shrugged, pretending that I didn't care. "He called me one of your whores. I didn't mean to slap him. It just happened. I'm sorry."

"Don't apologize, Claire. He shouldn't have called you that. Cooper has been rather…hard to handle, especially after Marie's death. This past year has been hell."

"He's an asshole," I muttered.

Robert grinned. "He can be, yes. Cooper and I have never really gotten along. He was always closer to Marie. The only reason he's living with me while he attends WVU is because he knows that's what she'd want. She forced him to stay with us his freshman year instead of moving into a dorm. I've spent the last year trying to reconnect with him, but he doesn't want anything to do with me."

"I didn't think he would be older than me, Robert. Why didn't you tell me?"

He shrugged. "It never came up. I didn't think it was a big deal."

"It's kind of creepy," I said.

He frowned. "I should've told you. For that, I'm sorry." He paused and glanced down at the dress clutched tightly to my chest.

"Claire, why are you in your underwear?"

"I decided to go for a swim. I didn't think anyone would see me."

He laughed, but I really didn't find it funny at all.

When I woke up to get ready for work the next morning, my first thought was of Cooper and the hurtful things he'd said to me. Robert's son was one of the coldest people I'd ever met, and that was saying something. He'd looked at me like he thought I was trash, like I was nothing, and that hurt. I hadn't done anything to cause him to assume the worst of me. Yes, wearing only my underwear probably hadn't helped my case any, but it wasn't like I'd known he was going to show up.

I grabbed my clothes and headed for the bathroom. In the hallway, my eyes never left Cooper's door. I was terrified that he'd appear from behind it. When I was safely inside the bathroom, I made sure that the door was locked before pulling my clothes off and turning on the water. All I'd need was for him to walk in on me, thinking that I'd left the door unlocked intentionally. That would really seal the deal in his eyes.

I showered quickly. Once I finished toweling off, I put on my clothes and dried my hair before pulling it up into a ponytail. Then, I cautiously opened the bathroom door. I sighed in relief when I saw that Cooper's door was still closed. I didn't want to deal with him today.

I stopped in my room to grab my purse and the keys to Robert's car before heading to the garage. Once I climbed inside the car, I rested my head against the seat and closed my eyes.

My new life with Robert kept growing more and more complicated. Being with him was supposed to make things easier. Instead, I felt like I had to constantly be on guard around him, and now, it would be the same with his son.

I opened my eyes and shoved the key in the ignition. The ring on my left hand caught my eye, and I paused. I stared at it, still trying to process the fact that something so beautiful really belonged to me. I twirled it around my finger, watching it shine in the sunlight coming through the window in the garage.

It still didn't seem real that I would be marrying Robert after such a short time knowing him. He was a good man, and he'd said he loved me. I couldn't help but feel uneasy about the situation as a whole.

I shook it off. I was being stupid. An incredible life had fallen into my lap, and here I was, debating on whether or not I was doing the right thing.

Robert would take care of me, and I knew that I could love him completely if I had enough time. That was all I needed—time. It was too bad that time had been in such short supply lately.

Work had been busier than normal. Usually, we were swamped in the summertime anyway, but today had just been ridiculous. I'd barely had time to talk to Junie or Sarah as we'd passed each other on the way to and from the kitchen. By the time our shift was over, I could tell they were just as desperate to escape as I was.

I watched the afternoon shift stare at the insanely busy diner before the servers grudgingly walked toward their tables. Once they took over, Junie, Sarah, and I headed to the back room to grab our things.

"I feel like I've been ridden hard and put away wet," Sarah grumbled as she snatched her purse out of the locker next to mine.

I laughed out loud at her crassness. "Good Lord, you really say whatever comes to mind, don't you?"

"Of course. Why would I ever keep my thoughts from others? They deserve to hear them, too." She stuck her tongue out at me.

I shoved some of my hair that had escaped my ponytail behind my ear. "All I want to do is sleep."

"Oh my God!" Sarah screamed, grabbing my hand and pulling it closer to her face. "Is that what I think it is?"

I snatched my hand away from her, trying to hide my engagement ring, but it was no use. She'd already seen it.

"Is it?" she asked when I didn't reply.

"Um…yeah, it is," I finally said, glancing over at Junie.

Her mouth was hanging open in shock.

"Ah! This is so exciting, Claire! Why didn't you tell us?" Sarah asked.

Junie looked away.

I shrugged. "It just happened last night, so I'm still trying to process it. Besides, we've been too busy to really talk today."

"I told you that he would have a ring on your finger before long! That man is head over heels for you, babe."

I smiled. "Yeah, you're right. I really care about him, and he treats me like gold, Sarah. I've never had someone pay attention to me the way he does."

"You're so lucky. I wish I could find some rich dude to fall in love with me. Sadly, the only guys I attract are broke assholes."

I laughed as she continued to complain about the men she'd dated. Hearing her horror stories made me realize just how lucky I was to be with Robert. I'd needed to talk to someone like this. Sarah's excitement calmed my nerves. I had made the right decision. I was doing the right thing.

I made a quick stop to Bob's office on my way out to let him know that I would no longer be staying in his office at the gym. He seemed surprised that I'd moved in with my boyfriend, but only wished me well. The girls had waited outside of his office and I met them at the door to leave together.

After chatting together for a few more minutes, Sarah waved at Junie and me as she headed to her car on the opposite side of the parking lot. I'd parked next to Junie this morning, so we walked across the lot together. I glanced over at her, but she refused to meet my eyes. She hadn't said a word about the ring on my finger, but I had a good idea of what she was thinking. Junie had never approved of Robert, and now that I was engaged to him, I doubted if she had changed her mind.

I mumbled a good-bye to her as I headed to where my car was parked. I was surprised when she called my name. I turned back around to see her standing where I'd left her.

"Yeah?" I asked.

"Do you love him?" she whispered the words, but she might as well have shouted them at me.

I flinched before I could stop myself. "I care a lot about him, Junie."

"But you don't love him," she said.

"I won't hurt him."

She looked at me, sadness filling her eyes. "I never said you would. It's not you that I'm worried about, Claire. Men like Robert don't think like the rest of us. He's rich and powerful. He didn't get that way by being a nice guy. I just don't want you to be played or hurt by him. Please think about that before you go through with this."

The pain in her voice made me wonder just who her ex-husband was. All I knew about him was his name—Jack. Anytime she'd

125

mentioned her divorce, I had sensed her pain, and I hadn't wanted to pry and cause her more anguish. Now, I felt like I needed to know.

Before I could ask her any of the questions burning through my mind, she was already in her car and pulling away from me.

I was surprised to see that Robert's car wasn't in the garage when I arrived home. He'd mentioned the night before that he would be home early. I checked my phone, noting that I had no missed calls or texts from him either.

I shrugged it off as I climbed out of the car and headed inside. He had probably ended up working later than he planned or had errands he needed to take care of. *Maybe he's trying to arrange our wedding,* I thought grumpily.

The house was completely silent as I climbed the stairs and turned down the hallway to my room. I raised an eyebrow in surprise when I noticed my bedroom door was partially open. I always closed my door, probably out of habit from living with foster siblings for so long. I assumed that it must have been the maid who had left it open, which is why I stopped short when I walked into the room. The maid wasn't there, but someone was, and that someone was making himself comfortable on my bed.

"What are you doing in here?" I asked Cooper.

He looked up from the file folder in his lap and stretched. "I was just doing some light reading."

"In my room? On my bed?" I asked, disbelief coloring my voice.

"Well, I was kinda waiting on you to get home, too."

"Why?"

He held up the file folder. "I spent my afternoon getting to know you, Claire. I have to say, my dad leaves out the most interesting files. I saw it when I talked to him earlier, and I decided to grab it after he left."

I stepped closer to him and saw my name written on the top of the file. I reached out to take it from him, but he held it out of my reach.

"Give that to me," I demanded.

"Why? You already know everything that's in it," he taunted. "It's *your* file after all."

"Give it to me!" I reached for it again.

This time, he held it out to me. "Wow, someone's grumpy today." He sat up.

I glared at him. I opened the folder and started reading through the papers inside. I couldn't believe just how much information there was. Robert had everything—medical records, dental records, my high school transcript, a list of every foster home I'd lived in. He even had information on my mother's death and the actual notes my CPS worker had written about me over the years. I flipped through more pages, and my mouth dropped open in shock. He had a detailed account of the night with Jason that I tried so hard to forget. There was even a piece of paper listing my prior boyfriends, which had the least amount of ink on it.

"Oh my God." I sank down onto the floor.

"It seems my dad had you thoroughly investigated before he let you into the house." Cooper paused. "I have to say, I thought your file would be different."

"Why?"

"Well, I figured your boyfriend list would be longer. I also expected something along the lines of *gold-digging whore* to pop up. But no, your life is nothing like I expected. *You* are nothing like I expected."

"Sorry to disappoint you!" I snapped, unable to keep my composure any longer. I knew Robert had said he'd checked into my background, but I'd never thought that he'd dug this deep.

"I'm not disappointed. I'm just surprised. I guess I now see what my dad sees in you."

"And what's that? Let me guess—a charity case. You both feel bad for me, right?" It bothered me that both Robert and Cooper knew every detail of my life.

"I do feel bad for you, but that's not what I'm talking about. I know how bad it hurts to lose your mom, and I'm sorry that you lost yours. I'm also sorry you had to grow up in the system. Just by reading your file, I can tell that you've had a rough life. But I also noticed something else. No matter which house you were in, CPS almost always noted how you would take care of the other kids. I expected you to be here because of my dad's money, but I don't think that's the case. You wouldn't still be working your shitty waitress job if you were. You would've quit the second you moved in here. I know why my father is so drawn to you, Claire. You're innocent and naive, and that's perfect for what he wants in a wife. He can shape you into whatever he wants, and then he can control you."

"What are you talking about?" I demanded.

"You've only seen one side of my father. He has plenty more sides, I promise, and I have no doubt that he'll show them once you're stuck with him in a sham of a marriage. He needs a pretty face, someone who will do whatever he wants with only a little persuasion, and that's you, wrapped up in a nice little package with a bow on top."

"It's good to know you think so highly of me, Cooper." I glared at him.

"Hey, I think more of you now than I did last night when I saw you wet and nearly naked. Speaking of that little outfit, I had some awesome dreams last night." He smirked at me before continuing, "You've had a shit life, Claire, so let me give you a little advice. Run like hell. The life you are walking into will be far worse than what you're walking away from."

"You know nothing about me. Your father makes me happy, and I haven't felt that way in a really long time. He *loves* me."

He laughed. "Just like I said, you're naive. My father doesn't love anyone but himself."

"You're telling me all this just to tear us apart. He told me about your relationship with him, Cooper. I'm not stupid. I know you've had a hard time since you lost your mom, but you have no right to take your anger out on me!"

He stood so fast that it barely registered in my mind. He crouched down on the floor next to me and glared. "This has *nothing* to do with my mother or my relationship with my dad. This is about you. I'm trying to keep you from making the biggest mistake of your life. He will destroy you. This is the one and only time I'm going to try to help you. Get the hell out of this house, and never look back. Once you say *I do*, it'll be too late."

I watched in silence as he stood and walked out of my room before slamming the door behind him. I pulled my knees up to my chest and rested my forehead against them.

Cooper is lying. He has to be.

That was the only reason I could think of that would have made him say those things to me. He hadn't really wanted to help me. He hated his father. Cooper had lied to hurt us both.

I refused to let my mind even begin to contemplate the idea that Cooper might be telling the truth.

Between Junie's and Cooper's warnings, Sarah's excitement, and Robert's soothing words, I felt like I was being ripped apart. I wasn't sure which way to turn anymore. I wished my mom were around to give me advice. It was too bad that was impossible—just like the situation I found myself in.

Robert found me an hour later. I was still sitting on the floor with the file clutched tightly against me when he walked in. He saw the file in my hands, and his eyes grew cold with fury.

"Where did you get that? Were you in my office?" he demanded.

I shook my head as I held it up to him. "Cooper."

He cursed before taking the folder and tossing it on my dresser. He leaned down and scooped me off the floor. I curled into his chest as he carried me down the hall and into his room. I glanced around briefly, taking in my surroundings. I'd never been in Robert's room before. His bed sat off to the left. It was the biggest bed I'd ever seen. The headboard and footboard were made from a dark wood. He had a matching dresser across the room from it. Two doors were on the right side of the room. I assumed one led to his closet, and the other had to go into his office since I hadn't found it anywhere else in the house.

He laid me down on his bed, and it felt like heaven. He climbed into bed behind me, and my body relaxed into his.

"Whatever he said to you, don't listen to him. I'm sorry, Claire. I thought I'd dealt with him today, but obviously, that wasn't the case. I'll have him out of here by next week."

"No, don't do that. He's your son, Robert. You can't just kick him out."

He muttered something under his breath that sounded like, *I wish he weren't*. Finally speaking to me again, he asked, "What did he say to you?"

"Nothing really. He just went over all the information you'd gathered on me," I lied. I wasn't sure why I had lied for Cooper, but I had done it anyway. I didn't want him and Robert to fight anymore. I knew they didn't get along, but I wouldn't come between them.

"I'm sorry you had to read it. I was going to get rid of it. I called him into my office this afternoon to discuss you. He must have seen it on my desk and picked it up when I wasn't paying attention."

"I feel violated, Robert. I knew you'd looked into me, but seeing the file was a whole different matter." I closed my eyes, trying to block out the whole situation. If only it were that easy.

"I know, and I'm sorry that I hurt you, but we've talked about this before. You know I had to be sure of who you were."

I simply nodded, still not opening my eyes. I was tired from not only working, but also from my conversations with Junie and Cooper. All I wanted to do was sleep.

"I have something for you," Robert finally said when he realized I wasn't going to speak.

It took everything in me not to groan. I was tired of getting presents, especially after I'd explained to him that I didn't want them.

"What?" I asked.

"Open your eyes and see," Robert coaxed.

I opened my eyes to see his hand holding a debit card in front of me. I rolled over to face him. "What's that?"

"A bank card." He gave me a duh look.

"Why do I need that? I already have one."

He sighed. "I had your old account closed and added you on one of mine. I transferred all your funds along with the money I got from selling your car into this one. I also put in a couple grand. If you need more, all you have to do is ask."

"You closed my bank account? How is that even possible? Only I can close it!"

He smiled. "I know the manager, and since I was transferring the money into another account with your name on it, he didn't mind helping me out."

"I…you…" I started, but I couldn't find the right words.

Once again, he was taking over my life. My bank account hadn't had much in it, but at least it had been mine. Now, it was gone, and in its place was an account with his name on it, too.

"I figured it would be easier this way. With my name on the account, I can easily transfer funds."

"I don't even know what to say," I said, barely hiding my anger.

He kissed my forehead. "You don't have to say anything. You're welcome, Claire. Also, I talked to your boss a little while ago."

My entire body tensed. "About what?"

"I explained that you needed all of next week and the following week off. He was upset because he's going to be a person short, and I suggested that he hire someone to take your place. We talked for a bit and decided that since he couldn't hire a person for only a couple of weeks, you don't have to go back. You're free, Claire."

I felt anything but free. "Come again?" I asked.

"You don't have to work there anymore. He's going to call a few people who put applications in before. Aren't you excited to finally be free of that place?"

"No, I'm *not* excited! I have to call him before he hires someone else!"

I sat up and tried to stand, but Robert held me down on the bed.

"Why would you do that?"

"Because I like working there!"

"You're being ridiculous! You're not going back there!"

I finally freed myself from his grip and jumped out of the bed. I ran to the door and threw it open. I hurried to my room and grabbed the cell phone Robert had paid for. I dialed the diner's number and waited for someone to pick up.

When Bob answered, I sighed in relief.

"Bob, it's Claire."

I saw Robert walking into my room, but I ignored him.

"Hey, Claire."

"Look, I know you talked to Robert today, but there's been a misunderstanding. I don't want to quit my job." When Bob didn't reply, I spoke again, "Bob? Are you still there?"

"I'm sorry, Claire, but I already hired someone to take your place. Robert said you wanted to quit because you wouldn't have time to work anymore."

"Call that person back and say the position has been filled already, Bob! I don't want to lose my job!"

"I can't, Claire. I'm really sorry." He paused. "I'm happy for you. I'm glad you found someone you love."

The call disconnected before I could reply. Defeated, I tossed my phone onto the bed. Anger simmered under my skin, begging to escape. I turned to Robert and glared at him.

I exploded when I saw the smug grin on his lips. "How could you do that to me, Robert? I loved working there! You had no right!"

"I had every right, Claire. You have no reason to work there anymore. It doesn't matter now. What's done is done. All we can do is move forward."

"Get out!" I shouted.

His eyes widened. "Excuse me?"

"You heard me. Get out of my room. I don't want to see you right now."

"Claire—"

"Out!" I screamed.

I knew Cooper was probably listening to every word I'd shouted, but I didn't care at the moment. I was too mad.

Robert glared at me for a minute before turning and walking out of my room. The door slammed behind him, like it had when Cooper left earlier.

"Fuck you!" I said as I glared at the door. *How dare he do this to me!*

I didn't speak to Robert for the rest of the night. Instead, I stayed in my room and shot dirty looks at everything within sight as Cooper's words played over and over in my mind.

You're innocent and naive, and that's perfect for what he wants in a wife. He can shape you into whatever he wants, and then he can control you.

I couldn't help but wonder if Cooper was right. Robert had been trying to control everything in my life—from my clothes to my bank account to my job. Nothing was mine anymore. If I left him now, I would have absolutely nothing. I would be worse off than I was when I'd moved in with him.

You're trapped, a voice whispered in my mind, *and he knows it.*

I had no idea what to do. I couldn't leave him, but I wasn't sure if I wanted to stay anymore.

I knew I wouldn't leave him. The thought of being on the streets with no car, no home, no job, and no money terrified me. It would be far worse than any foster home I'd stayed in.

"Goddamn it!" I shouted at no one in particular.

I took a deep breath to calm myself. I had to stay calm, or I would never figure anything out.

Maybe I was overreacting about everything. Maybe I'd let Cooper's words taint my outlook on my new life. He'd told me he was only trying to help, but after his little speech by the pool when he'd literally called me a whore, I doubted that. He didn't give a damn about me. He'd probably have a party if I left like he wanted.

I had to stay in control of the situation, no matter how lost I felt. I had no one but myself to blame for my current predicament, and no one would help me get out of it. As always, I was on my own.

I stood and walked across the room to my walk-in closet. I flipped on the light and peered inside. As I looked around at all the pretty clothes, I couldn't help but wonder what was so bad about letting Robert stay in control. Yes, it was annoying, but at the same time, I had everything I'd ever wanted out of life. If I stayed, my life would only get better even if I did feel trapped.

I turned and walked back to my bed. I dropped down onto it as I thought about my options. There were really only two—leave or stay. Leaving meant losing everything. Staying meant I would have everything I wanted, but I would be at Robert's mercy, totally and completely.

Could I let him control everything?

Stay and take what you want. You deserve it, a selfish voice whispered inside my mind. *You've always been kind to others, even when you were tossed aside time and time again. Take it, and never look back.*

"Never look back," I whispered.

I awoke to the sound of my bedroom door closing. I lay still as I strained my ears for the sound of someone moving around my room. When I heard nothing, I slowly pried my eyes open and glanced around. I gasped in shock as I stared around my room. Every surface and even parts of the floor were covered in roses—red roses, pink roses, yellow roses, white roses, and even multicolored roses. Everywhere I looked, there they were.

I took a deep breath, letting the floral scent invade my senses. I had no idea how I hadn't noticed it before.

I stood slowly and looked around at dozens upon dozens of roses. "Dear Lord," I whispered, still in shock.

I knew who they were from—Robert. He was trying to apologize for what had happened yesterday evening.

My decision to stay was the right choice. I would be a fool to leave someone who cared about me the way Robert did. Judging by the amount of flowers surrounding me, I knew he was truly sorry for overstepping his boundaries.

I walked to my dresser and pulled out sweatpants and a tank top along with a bra and underwear. I was careful not to knock any of the roses over as I crossed my room and opened the door. I headed toward the bathroom, not bothering to glance at Cooper's door this time. No matter what he said, I wouldn't listen to him. He had been toying with me, hoping to hurt not only me, but his father as well. It had almost worked yesterday, but I wouldn't fall for his act again. I was going to make this life with Robert work.

After a quick shower, I headed downstairs in search of Robert. I found him sitting at the dining room table, which was covered in food—eggs, bacon, hash browns, pancakes, waffles, turkey bacon, bagels, and a few other breakfast items. He was really pulling out all the stops today.

"Claire," he said as soon as he saw me. He stood and walked over to where I was standing. "I'm so sorry for what happened yesterday."

I stayed silent as he pulled me into his arms and held me tight. After a moment's hesitation, I wrapped my arms around him. He held me a few seconds longer before releasing me and stepping back.

"Please forgive me, Claire. I only want what's best for you." He stared down at me.

"I forgive you, Robert," I said.

He opened his mouth to reply, but he clamped it shut as a look of disbelief covered his face. "You do?"

He'd obviously expected me to make things harder for him. I gave him a weak smile, trying to reassure not only him, but myself as well.

"I know you were only trying to help, but next time, talk to me before you pull a stunt like that."

"I will. I promise. Did you enjoy your flowers?"

"I did. Thank you. They were lovely."

"Not as lovely as you." He took my hand and pulled me to the table. "I had my maid make breakfast for us. Eat whatever you want."

We sat down, our hands still linked.

"You didn't have to do all this, Robert."

"I know I didn't have to. I wanted to."

"Well, I appreciate it," I said quietly as I put some eggs and bacon on my plate.

After a few minutes of silence while we ate, Robert finally spoke, "I have some bad news."

I swallowed my food before looking up at him. At this point, I was afraid to even ask, "What is it?"

"I was contacted about a case last night. It's huge, and there's no way I can pass it up."

"Okay…" I said, still confused as to where he was going with this.

"We're going to have to push our marriage back for a couple of weeks. I'm so sorry, Claire, but I can't let this one go."

I was shocked at the relief I felt at his words. *I still have time. Thank you, Lord.* "I understand. I want to be honest with you. I'm kind of relieved that we have to postpone things."

"Why are you relieved?" he asked.

"Because we're moving too fast. This will give us some time to get used to living together and being a part of each other's daily lives."

He seemed to consider my words. "I think you're right. I've pushed you into this, haven't I?"

I sighed. I was relieved that he'd understood what I had been trying to tell him, and he hadn't gotten upset.

"A little bit. It's not that I don't care about you, Robert, because I do. It's just that we're moving so fast."

He nodded. "You're right. Sometimes, I forget to think about others. I only focus on what I want."

I reached for his hand and squeezed it lightly. "This will be good for both of us. I can feel it."

He smiled. "I wanted to talk to you about something else as well."

"What is it?"

He sighed. "I don't know how to say this without sounding like an ass, so I'm just going to spit it out. I want you to start sleeping in my room with me."

My eyes widened in surprise. "Oh."

"I want you in my bed, Claire. It drives me crazy to know you're so close, yet you're still so very far away from me. I've been patient with you because I know your history, but it's been a long time since I've been with anyone. I *need* you."

I felt my cheeks turn red from embarrassment. "I don't know what to say."

"Say you'll stay with me. I promise we'll take our time. You have nothing to fear from me."

I couldn't believe we were sitting here, eating breakfast, and talking about our potential sex life. I stared at Robert, debating on what to do. I was attracted to him—that much was obvious to me—but I'd never really cared about sex. My one and only time had been with a boy I dated in high school, and it was nothing to brag about.

You're engaged to the man. Why didn't you factor sex in, idiot?

"I'll stay with you," I said quietly.

He smiled. "Thank God. I wasn't above begging."

I closed my eyes as he leaned over and kissed me softly. I tried to lose myself in the kiss, but all I could think about was the fact that I'd just agreed to have sex with Robert. That was another huge step that I would be taking with him.

"I'll have Ellie move your things into my room today. You don't have to do anything." He kissed me again before pulling away and standing. "I have to go to my office for a bit. I'll be back later though."

"Okay." I watched him walk away.

I looked down at my almost full plate of food and pushed it away. I was no longer hungry. My stomach was too full of butterflies to fit any actual food in there.

I kept repeating to myself, *This is my choice. I can do this. I want this. Everything will be just fine.*

Despite Robert's assurance that I wouldn't have to help the maid move all my belongings to his room, I still felt that I should help.

I met Ellie, Robert's maid, in the kitchen. She seemed surprised to see me there, but once we started talking, she was very friendly. She insisted that I didn't need to help her clean up breakfast, but I ignored her as I wrapped the uneaten food and stuck it in the fridge.

Ellie was older, probably in her early sixties. She was tiny, even compared to me. I doubted if she was five feet. Her gray hair was cut short, the way most older women wore it. Everything about her screamed dainty and fragile.

Once breakfast was put away and the dishwasher was running, we headed up to my room to start moving all my belongings to Robert's room. After several trips back and forth, we had most of my clothes in his closet. The rest would have to stay in my room since his closet was now full. It felt strange to see my clothes next to his. It made everything more real to me.

After Ellie and I finished moving my things, I followed her around the house as she cleaned and did laundry. The only time I didn't follow her was when she had to go into Cooper's room. I hadn't seen him yet today, and I hoped I wouldn't.

Ellie chatted about her grandkids as she worked, and she even showed me pictures of them. She had two, Emily and Evan, who were five-year-old twins. They were the cutest kids I'd ever seen. Both had bright red hair and a face full of freckles. Ellie told me that they spent every weekend with her. I laughed when she said she always filled them with candy on Sunday before sending them back to their parents.

I was sad when it was time for Ellie to leave. It had been nice to have someone to talk to in the house. I also liked the fact that Ellie hadn't made a single comment about the fact that I was moving into Robert's room. She obviously knew I was his girlfriend, but she'd kept her thoughts to herself. I appreciated that more than she could know. It had seemed like everyone had an opinion when it came to my relationship with him, and it was refreshing to hear nothing.

After Ellie left, I spent the rest of my day reading by the pool. I had to admit, having an e-reader was probably the coolest thing ever. I had millions of books right at my fingertips. Once the sun started to set, I put my e-reader down and closed my eyes.

It seemed like just minutes had passed when I felt someone gently pushing on my shoulder. I opened my eyes slowly to see Robert standing beside me.

I gave him a sheepish smile. "Sorry. I guess I fell asleep."

"It's okay. I got home a few minutes ago. I couldn't find you, so I figured you were out here."

I sat up and stretched. "Did you have a good day at work?"

He nodded. "A very good day. The case I mentioned is going to require a lot of work, but I have no doubt that I can win it."

"What kind of case is it?" I asked.

"Don't worry about it. Come on, let's get you inside."

I frowned as I stood up. Robert never gave me much information on any of his cases. He would mention them briefly, but when I asked for more, he'd brush me off. I knew he couldn't tell me a lot about them, but he could tell me something, anything. I wanted to be a part of his life, and that included his job. I felt as if he thought I wasn't capable of having a serious conversation about his work, or maybe he thought I wouldn't be able to grasp it. That thought hurt more than I'd expected.

"I meant to tell you earlier that we're going to a function tomorrow night." Robert took my hand and led me inside.

"What kind of function?" I asked.

"Every few months, some of the lawyers in town get together. Last time, I held the party here, but my friend and colleague, Brad, is throwing it this time. It's formal. You should be able to find something nice to wear."

I couldn't help but feel nervous over the fact that I would be meeting his colleagues. "Why do I need to go?"

He looked at me as if I'd lost my mind. "Why wouldn't you?"

I shrugged. "I don't know. It's just that you've never really brought me to anything like this before."

"We weren't engaged before. It's time my colleagues finally meet my future wife. I won't lie. I can't wait to show you off," he said as we climbed the stairs and turned toward his room.

I couldn't help but feel a sense of pride at his words. He was proud of me, and he wanted his friends to meet me. I forced my nerves away. I knew that I'd have to meet them eventually, so I might as well get it over with before we were married.

"Do you think they'll like me?" I asked.

"I have no doubt that they will. I'm sure they'll be shocked to learn that I'm engaged, but once they talk to you, they'll understand why I love you so much."

I smiled as we walked into his room. "You know, you can be sweet when you want to be."

He closed the door behind us and turned to me. Before I could blink, he had me pressed up against the wall.

"Is that so?" he asked quietly.

My nerves returned instantly, but it was for a whole new reason. His body pressed into mine, and I felt his erection against my thigh. He was already turned-on, and we'd just walked in. I had no doubt about where this night would lead.

"Yes," I whispered.

He leaned in and kissed me softly. "I've pictured you in my bed all day, Claire."

I gazed up at him, my stomach in knots. "Is that so?"

"Definitely. I know you're nervous, but I promise you'll enjoy yourself."

He leaned down and kissed me again as his hand slid under my shirt. I shuddered as desire began to build inside me. God, I was so scared, but I wanted him, too. I wanted to feel loved, and I knew he'd take care of me.

Slowly, I pulled his shirt out of his pants and started unbuttoning it. Once the last button was undone, I slid it off of his shoulders and ran my hands down his bare chest. He moaned into my mouth as he pressed his hips against mine.

"I love your hands on me," he whispered after he broke our kiss.

He grabbed the bottom of my shirt and tugged it over my head. Next, he pulled the string on my pants and shoved them down my hips. He stepped away so that I could kick them off.

He picked me up and carried me over to the bed. He laid me down on top of the covers and stared down at me. I had the sudden urge to cover myself, but I refrained. He smiled as he undid his belt and then the button on his pants. I watched as he took them off and climbed into bed.

His body looked just as amazing as I had expected. I only had a second to glance at it before he leaned down and kissed me, but it was enough time to know just how lucky I was. He continued to kiss me for a few minutes before pulling away again.

"Are you on birth control?" he asked.

I shook my head. "No, I haven't…done this in a really long time."

"It's okay. I'll call the doctor tomorrow and set up an appointment for you. Until then, we'll use protection."

He leaned over and opened a drawer in his nightstand. He pulled a condom out before closing the drawer. I watched with rapt attention as he stood and removed his boxers. I bit my lip as I stared at his cock. The one and only time I'd had sex, it had been in the dark. I blushed as I realized I'd never seen one before. God, I was so innocent compared to him. He'd spent years with his wife. How could I compare to her?

No, don't think about her, I chastised myself. *You can't compare yourself to her. What they had was special, but she's gone now, and he wants you.*

He climbed back into bed and lifted me so that he could unsnap my bra. Once it was free, he pulled it off and tossed it onto the floor. He stared at my breasts with an animalistic desire in his eyes. His gaze slowly traveled down my body to my underwear. He reached down and tugged on them. I raised my hips, and his fingers slipped them down my legs before I kicked them off. We stared at each other, both of us completely naked. I'd never felt so vulnerable in my life. Robert was finally seeing me like this.

"God, Claire, you're perfect," he whispered. He slid his hand up my stomach until he was cupping one of my breasts. "So beautiful."

My breath hitched as he pinched my nipple between his finger and thumb. Tingles shot through my body, all of them landing in one spot. I rubbed my legs together as my core began to ache.

Robert released my breast, and he ripped the package open before rolling the condom on. I watched in fascination. Once it was on, his body covered mine, and he kissed me deeply. For the first time, I felt something from his kiss. That feeling alone brought me so much joy that I was momentarily stunned.

I was brought out of my stupor when Robert thrust into me. I cried out in shock and pain as my body tried to adjust to his size.

"God, you're so tight." Robert pulled out and then began thrusting into me.

I closed my eyes and waited for the pain to fade. Finally, it did, and I was able to move with him. My hips rose to meet his, and I felt my body building with pleasure. I gripped his shoulders as his thrusts became harder and more erratic. Suddenly, he shouted incoherently as he released into me. I expected him to continue pumping into me, so I could find my own release, but he stopped and dropped his head onto my shoulder.

"That was incredible, Claire," he said once his breathing had returned to normal.

"Yeah, incredible," I said.

He pulled out and stood. I watched as he removed the condom and tossed it into the trash. He scooted me over and pulled the sheets down on his side of the bed.

After he climbed in, he turned to me and smiled. "Good night, Claire."

"Good night," I whispered as I watched him close his eyes.

He was asleep within minutes. Once I was sure he was asleep, I stood and redressed before pulling the sheets down and climbing in next to him.

I stared up at the ceiling, knowing that sleep was nowhere to be found for me. My body was still trying to understand what had just happened, and my mind was going in twenty different directions.

What just happened? I expected…more from sex.

I'd thought it would be different this time. I'd thought I would enjoy it. In high school, I'd heard so many girls talk about sex, telling each other how amazing it was.

Maybe I had expected too much, or maybe I was broken.

That has to be it. Great, my vagina is broken. I snorted out loud at the thought alone.

Finally, I drifted off to sleep, my dreams filled with broken vaginas. *Awesome.*

When I woke up the next morning, Robert was gone. In his place was a note, letting me know that I needed to be ready for the party at five. He'd had to go to work, but he would pick me up tonight.

I climbed out of bed, feeling sore between my legs. I frowned as I walked to the dresser and opened the one drawer I had. I pulled out a pair of black shorts, a tank top, and underwear. I opened the door and walked across the hall to the bathroom. After a quick shower, I made my way to the kitchen to find something to eat.

I was surprised when I saw Cooper sitting at the kitchen table, eating a bowl of cereal. He normally didn't show his face around the house—at least not when I was around. He looked up when I entered and gave me a smirk. I ignored him as I walked to the pantry and pulled out a box of cereal. I grabbed a bowl and a spoon before walking to the fridge to get a carton of milk.

After I poured the cereal and milk into the bowl and put everything away, I stood by the counter, unsure of what to do. I really didn't want to sit down and eat breakfast with Cooper. I didn't even want to be in the same room as him. I shifted from foot to foot as I debated on what to do. I decided I'd rather eat in Robert's room than be near Cooper. I picked up my bowl and headed for the door.

"You can eat with me, you know. I won't bite," Cooper said.

I stopped and turned around to face him. I didn't even try to hide my frown. "Why would I sit with you? I'd rather eat in my room than have to deal with you being an asshole."

I couldn't stop my eyes from trailing over him. I cursed myself as I took in his still damp hair and tight tank top. Obviously, the boy didn't own an actual shirt. I hated the way my body responded to the sight of him. Someone who was such an asshole shouldn't be allowed to look that good.

He laughed. "I promise, I'll be on my best behavior."

"I'm sure you will," I muttered as I walked across the kitchen and sat down across from him.

I started eating my cereal, very much aware of the fact that Cooper was staring at me. I tried to ignore him, but after a few minutes, I finally gave up and looked at him.

"Why do you keep watching me?" I snapped.

Obviously, I'd woken up on the wrong side of the bed this morning. *Or the wrong bed—period.*

"Am I bothering you?" he asked, ignoring my question.

"Yes, you are. It's kind of hard to eat when I can feel you watching my every move."

"What can I say, Claire? I find you interesting."

"I doubt that," I muttered.

He grinned. "Someone woke up cranky this morning. I bet you didn't get much sleep last night, did you? I heard my dad getting his rocks off, and I'm pretty sure you helped him with that since you stayed in his room. Just so you know, it's kind of disgusting for me to wake up and hear that."

My face warmed in embarrassment. "That's none of your business, Cooper."

He chuckled. "You really are nothing like I expected. Look at you. Your face is on fire."

"You're being crude. Of course it's going to embarrass me!" I glared at him.

"I'm not being crude. I'm just pointing out the fact that you're having very vocal sex with my dad." He paused. "You know, I heard *him* last night, but I never heard you. I find that kind of strange."

I looked away from him and started shoving cereal into my mouth again. He was baiting me, hoping to either make me angry or make me talk. I refused to do either.

"I have two theories on why I didn't hear you. The first one is, you're just quiet during sex. I somehow doubt that though since most women are very…vocal when they're getting off. The second theory is my favorite. Do you want to know what it is?"

I ignored him, and he laughed.

"Come on, I know you're curious. I'll tell you anyway even though you didn't ask. I think the reason I never heard a peep from you was because you didn't get off. Am I right? Did dear old Dad get off and leave you hanging? I bet he did. You must be so frustrated this morning. That's probably why you're so cranky. It isn't from your lack of sleep. It's from your lack of the big O."

"You're an ass." I glared daggers at him.

"Oh, touchy. I must be right. If you want, I can talk to my dad for you and give him some pointers on how to make you scream like a crazy bitch."

"You're disgusting!" I shoved my chair back and stood.

He laughed as I turned and started to march out of the kitchen. My escape was halted when I met Ellie in the doorway. She smiled at me, but it slipped when she saw my face. She glanced behind me at Cooper, who was still laughing, before turning her attention back to me.

"Oh, dear," she mumbled. She cleared her throat and spoke louder as she said, "Cooper, what did you do to Claire?"

His laugh was cut off when he heard Ellie's voice. I glanced back to see that his face had lost all its humor.

"Good morning, Ellie," he said politely.

I wanted to roll my eyes at his tone. There was nothing polite about Cooper.

"Don't *good morning, Ellie* me, Cooper. What did you do to Claire?" Ellie asked with a sternness that would have made any mother proud.

He had the decency to look embarrassed for a split second before he wiped the emotion off his face. "I was just joking with her, and she took it personally."

Ellie crossed her arms as her frown deepened. "You leave Claire alone, Coop. She's a nice girl. I won't have you running her off."

I raised an eyebrow at the nickname. If she had a nickname for him, she obviously liked the moron.

"Sorry, Ellie. It won't happen again."

Yeah, right.

I watched Cooper stand. He grabbed both our bowls and took them to the sink.

How domestic of him.

"It'd better not. Now, come over here and give me a hug. I haven't seen you since you got back." Ellie moved past me and walked into the kitchen.

Cooper smiled as he moved toward her and pulled her into his arms. "I missed you, Ellie."

"I missed you, too. Did you have a nice vacation?"

He nodded as they broke apart. "It was very nice."

"Good. Now, get out of here before I beat your behind. I have work to do." She turned to look at me again.

After watching Cooper act like a decent human being with Ellie, I was sure the look on my face was priceless.

"Robert said I needed to help you pick out something to wear tonight," Ellie said to me.

"What's happening tonight?" Cooper asked.

"Robert is taking her to one of those lawyer parties he goes to," Ellie said.

Cooper rolled his eyes before glancing at me. "You're going to be bored out of your mind."

"Stop annoying Claire, and get out of here, Cooper," Ellie said as she motioned toward the door.

"Fine. I can tell when I'm not wanted." Cooper walked toward me.

I was still standing in the doorway, but there was plenty of room for him to pass. He raised an eyebrow at me when I didn't move. After a moment, he shrugged and moved past me. As he stepped beside me, his chest pressed against my breasts. The tiny touch caused a bolt of lust to shoot through my body. Shocked at my reaction, I sucked in a breath. His body froze as he glanced down at me. Whatever he saw in my eyes made him smirk.

He pressed closer to me and lowered his lips so that they were only an inch from my ear. "You have fun at the party, *Claire*. Don't forget my offer. I'll be glad to talk to Dad for you."

His warm breath against my skin made me shudder, and I tried to hide it. I glared at him as he pulled back, and then he walked away. He glanced back at me once before heading upstairs.

"I don't know what I'm going to do with that boy," Ellie said once he was gone.

I looked over at her. "What do you mean?"

"He's so darn stubborn. He's a good boy, Claire, even though I'm sure he's hidden that from you."

I shrugged. "Cooper has been nothing but an asshole to me. I'm not worried about it though. It's not like he's a ten-year-old kid that I'll have to spend the next eight years raising. I don't care if he likes me or not."

"He'll warm up to you. Just give him some time. He comes off as an arrogant ass, but he's really not. Losing his mother changed him, made him colder. I understand why he is the way he is, but I hate that he pushes everyone away." Ellie sighed. "Anyway, let me get my chores finished up, and then I'll meet you in Robert's room. We need to find something for you to wear."

I nodded before turning and walking out of the kitchen. I hated that Ellie's words kept running through my mind. It would be much easier to ignore Cooper as long as he portrayed himself as an asshole.

Ellie knocked on Robert's door an hour later. After I let her in, she walked straight to the closet and started searching through some of the dresses we'd hung in there yesterday. I stayed silent as I watched her.

"None of these will do. Let's go see what's in your room," she said as she came out of the closet.

I followed her down the hall and into my old room. We searched through my old closet until she clapped her hands together.

She pulled out a dress and held it out to me. "This is the one! You'll look stunning in this."

I took it from her and looked it over. It was a black dress that would reach just above my knees. The front was modest, only showing off a peek of cleavage. The back was another story. Only a few strategically placed strings of material held the almost completely backless dress together. It was obvious that I'd have to skip a bra tonight.

"It's perfect. Thank you, Ellie." I smiled at her.

"Go try it on!" she said excitedly.

I nodded before walking out of the closet. Exiting my room, I headed to the bathroom and locked the door behind me. I stripped down until I was wearing only my underwear, and then I pulled the dress on. I looked at my refection in the mirror. The dress really was perfect. It fit my body like a glove, but it wasn't so tight that it looked trashy.

I walked back to my old bedroom where Ellie was waiting for me. Her face lit up as she stared at me. I did a silly little twirl in front of her, and we both laughed.

"It's gorgeous, Claire! Those lawyers will never know what hit them!" she said excitedly.

"You really think so?" I asked.

"I know so. They're going to take one look at you and fall in love. Once they actually talk to you, they'll want to steal you away from Robert."

I grinned. "You're the best, Ellie. I hope you know that."

"You're too sweet, Claire." She studied the dress for a minute. "Wear just a little bit of makeup and make sure to do your hair in some kind of updo. You'll be stunning."

"Okay, I will. I'm going to go change." I turned and walked out of the room.

Just as I reached the bathroom, I heard Cooper's door open. I froze for a second before glancing back at him. He was staring at me with his mouth hanging open. We stared at each other for a moment before I hurried into the bathroom and slammed the door closed. My hands were shaking, and I laughed at myself.

What is it about Cooper that makes me so damn nervous?

I shouldn't care about him at all. I shouldn't give him the power to make me nervous.

I forced myself not to think about him as I quickly took off the dress and changed back into my regular clothes. I made sure to hang the dress up on the back of the door so that it wouldn't wrinkle. I headed back out into the hallway. Cooper was nowhere to be seen, and I sighed in relief. I didn't want to deal with him for the rest of the day.

Ellie was standing outside my room, still smiling. "I need to head out, but I just wanted to tell you that you're going to do great tonight. You have no reason to be nervous."

"Thank you, Ellie. I mean it. It's nice to have someone like you around."

She smiled. "Don't let the Evans men scare you. If they do, I'll kick them both out."

We laughed together for a minute before she finally said good-bye and left.

Ellie was good for me. It was nice to have her around the house even if it was usually only for a few hours each day. I had no doubt that the longer I stayed here, the more attached I would grow to her.

Despite Ellie's reassuring words, I was still nervous when Robert picked me up that night. Suddenly, I began second-guessing not only the dress, but my hair as well. I climbed into the car, and by the look on his face, I knew that he approved of my dress.

I'd spent an ungodly amount of time getting ready. I'd showered and shaved before slathering almost every inch of my body with lotion. If all else failed, at least I knew I smelled good. Then, I'd applied my makeup. Remembering Ellie's suggestion, I'd used only minimal amounts.

My hair was another matter. I'd never been one of those girls who could make her hair look awesome with little effort. I'd spent almost two hours trying to get my hair into an updo that I thought would look both mature and flattering. I'd finally managed to get my hair into a French twist. I'd left a few strands down in front and curled them. I'd spent so long getting ready that I wasn't even dressed yet when Robert called to say that he'd be at the house in just a few minutes. I'd hurried to pull on my dress before grabbing a small black clutch and a pair of black heels. Then, I'd moved as fast as my heels would allow me down the stairs and out the front door.

Robert started driving. "You look wonderful, Claire."

We passed through the gate at the end of our driveway.

I looked him over. "Thank you. You do, too."

He was wearing a dark gray suit with a matching tie and a white dress shirt. By the way the suit fit his well-muscled body, it had obviously been custom-fitted to him.

"So, what is this party going to be like?" I asked.

"It'll mainly be about business, but you won't have to endure much of that. Most of the men will bring their wives or girlfriends. You can socialize with them while I talk business."

"Do you think they'll like me?" I played with the bottom of my dress.

"I'm sure they will. They all got along with Marie just fine."

My stomach sank. If they'd been friends with Marie, then there was a good chance that they wouldn't like me just because I was with her husband. I closed my eyes and willed myself to calm down. Maybe I was worrying too much. Maybe they'd welcome me with open arms. I sighed. That thought was almost laughable. They'd take one look at me and realize that I was nothing like them.

What could an eighteen-year-old foster kid have in common with a bunch of rich lawyers' wives?

It took us fifteen minutes to arrive at the party. We pulled up to Brad Buckhannon's house. In awe, I stared up at the massive home. It was three stories high and made of stone. There had to be at least a dozen windows in the front of the house, allowing light to spill out of the first two stories.

A man opened my door for me. I thanked him as I climbed out of the car, clutching my purse to my chest like it was a security blanket. Robert handed his car keys off to another man before wrapping his arm around me and leading me up the steps to the home. I clung to his arm, terrified that he'd leave me once we were inside.

As another man opened the front door for us, Robert gave me a brief smile. "Breathe, Claire. This is a party. You're supposed to have fun."

I nodded, but I didn't loosen my grip on his arm. Robert led us through the brightly lit foyer and into a room large enough to hold a small house.

Jesus, I thought as I looked around.

The floor was a dark marble, and the walls were a dark gray color. Every few feet, miniature chandeliers hung from the high ceiling.

I turned my attention from the room to the people inside. All the men were dressed in suits. I glanced at their faces, noting that most of them appeared to be older than Robert. They were standing around in groups, talking to each other, and ignoring the women on the other side of the room.

The women were dressed to the nines. Every single one of them was wearing a dress. I noticed a few of them glancing at Robert and me, but none of them approached. It took the men a little longer to notice us. Once they did, every single one of them gravitated toward us, their eyes glued to Robert.

"Robert! Glad you could make it," a middle-aged man said as he stopped in front of us. He glanced at me and smiled. "Who's this lovely lady?"

"This is Claire, my fiancée. Claire, this is my close friend, Brad. He's hosting the festivities this evening."

I noticed the way Brad's eyes widened at the word *fiancée*, but he managed to hide his surprise after that. I held out my hand, and Brad shook it. He was probably in his early fifties. He was shorter than Robert by at least three inches. His frame was rail thin, making it obvious that he didn't work out the way Robert did. Brad's smile was nice though, and it seemed sincere.

"Wow, you have been a busy boy, Robert. Where did you find such a beautiful young woman?"

Robert chuckled. "I'll never tell. I can't have you trying to find one of your own."

Brad laughed. "I would never do such a thing."

The rest of the men had gathered around us. I kept my eyes glued to the floor as Robert spoke to each of them. It seemed like all of them were practically begging for his attention, and it made me realize just how important Robert was.

"Robert, it's so good to see you again," a female voice said.

I looked up to see a pretty woman who appeared to be in her mid-thirties. She had dark red hair, and her skin was fair and blemish-free. Her hair was piled on her head in an updo that I would never be able to master. Her makeup was much more noticeable than mine with her dark red lipstick and heavy eye shadow.

She hugged Robert briefly before stepping away and looking at me. "Who's this, Robert? Did you get another secretary?"

I narrowed my eyes at her. Her question had been innocent enough, but it was her tone that had caught my attention. It had been filled with sarcasm and another emotion I couldn't identify, and I wasn't sure that I wanted to.

"Sandra, this is my fiancée, Claire," Robert said as he squeezed my hand.

Sandra raised an eyebrow in surprise. "Wow. Really? A little young for you, don't you think?"

"Sandra!" Brad said, his voice filled with annoyance. He gave Robert an apologetic look.

"Not at all," Robert said, apparently not bothered by her snide remark. "Claire's very special."

Sandra looked at me, no longer hiding her disdain. "I'm sure she is. If you'll excuse me, I have better people to talk to than someone like *her*."

My mouth dropped open in shock. Then, I got mad, really mad. Before I could stop myself, I said, "Excuse me, Sandra? What exactly is that supposed to mean?"

She laughed. "You really want me to spell it out for you? Fine, I will. Apparently, I'm the only one brave enough to say it, but I assure you, everyone in this room is thinking it. You're the type of girl who finds a rich older man and sinks her claws into him. Poor Marie has been gone just over a year, and Robert's already engaged to you. She'd roll over in her grave if she knew *you* were her replacement."

"How *dare* you!" I spit. "You know nothing about me!"

She snickered. "And I'd like to keep it that way. I don't associate with trash like you."

I stepped forward, determined to sink my claws into her. I didn't care who this woman was. She had no right to talk to me like that.

"You little—" I started to say before I was cut off.

Robert stepped in front of me, looking angry. I wasn't sure who he was angry with, Sandra or me. Maybe both. "Enough."

"Good boy, Robert. Keep your little toy in check." Sandra smiled cruelly.

With that, she spun on her heel and walked away. No one said a word. I looked up to see Robert glaring at Sandra, his face a deep shade of red. Tears of embarrassment and anger filled my eyes. I'd known that these people wouldn't take me in with open arms, but I'd never expected *this*.

"Robert, I'm sorry. I'll talk to her," Brad said, looking mortified.

Robert turned his glare toward Brad. "Get your bitch under control. I won't stand for this."

"I understand. It'll be taken care of." Brad looked at Sandra.

She was standing with a group of women. All of them were laughing before glancing over at us. I had a good idea about what they had been laughing about.

Robert looked around the room at all the men standing there. "If this ever happens again, I won't be back. I suggest you get your wives under control. There will be no second chances."

He turned, and with me in tow, he walked toward the door. I looked back when I heard someone following us. Brad was only a few feet behind us. I tugged on Robert's sleeve, but he shook his head. Once we were back in the foyer, he stopped and let Brad catch up with us.

"What, Brad?" Robert said, obviously annoyed.

"You don't need to leave, Robert. I'll take care of Sandra and anyone else who causes a problem."

Robert laughed. "Somehow, I doubt you will. Sandra has always been the one in control, and we both know it. I suggest you grow a pair of balls before you take on that bitch you call a wife."

My mouth dropped open in shock, and so did Brad's. Robert ignored him as he led me out of the foyer. We waited as one of Brad's men pulled our car around. I tried my hardest to dry my tears, but every few seconds, a new one would escape and slide down my face.

Robert didn't say a word until we were in the car and headed back to his house.

"Please don't cry, Claire. I never expected them to react like that, or I would've given them all a heads-up."

"It's not your fault," I whispered as I stared out the window.

I'd never felt so hurt in my entire life. I'd done nothing to Sandra or any of those other women. I hadn't even said a word to her until she'd attacked me. I had tried my hardest to fit in, and she hadn't even noticed. I'd worn this stupid dress and fixed my hair and makeup like Ellie had told me, and it still hadn't mattered. Sandra really would think I was trash if she knew how I'd grown up.

"Sandra has always been rather…difficult to handle. She was very close to Marie, and she obviously felt the need to remind me of her. Sandra's an ignorant bitch. Brad has let her get away with anything and everything but no more. If he doesn't handle her, I will."

"I should've known they wouldn't accept me." I turned to look at him. "I don't fit in, and I never will."

"Nonsense, Claire. You were the most beautiful woman there tonight. That's probably why she was so mad. Sandra has always been a vain woman, and she's always been the youngest. She feels threatened."

I snorted. "If that's her feeling threatened, I'd hate to see her truly mad."

Robert chuckled. "Don't worry about tonight, okay? The next event will be different. Those men are worried about what I'll do if they don't control their wives." He glanced at me and grinned. "They kiss my ass too much to let their wives screw up their plans."

"Why are you so important?" I was curious why men older than him had vied for his attention tonight.

"Because I've never lost a case—ever. I started practicing law as soon as I graduated from law school. Even then, I was a force to be reckoned with. Now that I own my firm with lawyers working under me, I'm almost unstoppable—not just in Morgantown, but in the entire state of West Virginia. I'm also about to open up a new firm in Pittsburgh, which will only help me further my carreer."

"Wow," I mumbled. This was the most information he'd given me about his work since we met. "I had no idea."

"Plus, I've made some rather powerful friends over the years, and they've helped me immensely. No one wants to piss me off."

"Are any of them really your friends? Or do they just want to use you?" I asked.

He frowned. "I don't really worry about friends, Claire, but Brad is probably the closest thing I have to a friend."

"But he's terrified of you," I said.

He laughed. "That's the best way to control people—keep them terrified of you. It's all politics, Claire."

I shook my head. "I'm glad I'm not a part of it. I couldn't stand to live like that."

We pulled up to the house. As soon as the car came to a stop in the garage, I climbed out and headed for the door leading into the house. Robert was right behind me. He kept his arm around my waist as we climbed the stairs and headed for our room.

I walked to the dresser and pulled out a pair of pajamas. I took my heels and dress off and tossed them into the corner of the closet. I put my pajamas on and climbed into bed. Robert did the same. Once we were situated under the covers, he pulled me to him. I snuggled up against him and let my body relax. I fell asleep before I could say another word.

I awoke to the sound of Robert's voice. I opened my eyes to see him sitting on the bed, talking quietly into his cell phone.

"You can't be serious. I'm just starting on a new case. I can't come up there right now," he said, his voice hushed.

He was silent for a few minutes as he listened to whoever was on the other end of the line.

He sighed loudly. "This is what I pay you for, Andrew." He paused. "Fine, I'll be there in a few hours."

He put his phone down on the nightstand and stood. He glanced back to see me watching him. "I didn't mean to wake you." He rubbed his eyes.

"Everything okay?" I asked.

"No. Remember me mentioning my expansion into Pittsburgh?"

I nodded.

"Well, there's a slight problem. I need to go to Pittsburgh for a couple of days."

"Oh," I said.

"I'm sorry to leave so suddenly, but it can't wait."

"It's okay. I understand." I smiled at him.

I watched from the bed as he packed a small suitcase. Then, he got dressed in a pair of slacks and a white button-down shirt.

"I'll call you when I arrive. If you need anything, you have my number." He kissed me on the forehead before heading for the door.

"I will."

I lay in bed for several minutes before finally convincing myself to get up. I grabbed an outfit and headed for the bathroom. Once inside, I took one look at myself and frowned. I looked like hell. I'd gone to bed with my hair still styled and my makeup still on. While I'd slept, my hair had come out of the French twist, and it now looked like a beehive on top of my head. I'd worn little makeup, but my eyeliner and mascara had smudged, so I now looked like a raccoon. It was no wonder Robert had been so desperate to leave this morning.

After I showered, I braided my wet hair to keep it out of my way. I pulled on one of my old T-shirts and a pair of cutoff jean shorts. I smiled at myself in the mirror. This was me, not the girl I'd pretended to be last night. When I'd been dressed like that, I'd felt like I was an actress playing a role, not an actual person.

I headed downstairs to the kitchen and grabbed a granola bar. I wasn't hungry, but I figured I might as well eat. As I munched on my breakfast, I leaned against the counter, trying to decide how I wanted to spend my day. It was strange not having to work every day. I missed my friends as well as my regular customers at the diner. I wanted to stop in to see them, but after my last conversation with Junie, I wasn't sure if that was a good idea or not.

My thoughts drifted to Shelly, the little girl I'd left behind when I was kicked out of Rick and Tammy's house. I wondered how she was doing. Without thinking, I pulled my phone out of my pocket and called their house. I was surprised that I still remembered the phone number. It wasn't like I'd called home all that often. If Rick's schedule was still the same, I knew he'd be at work, but Tammy might be home.

Sure enough, she picked up on the third ring. "Hello?" she answered cautiously, obviously not recognizing my number.

"Tammy?" I asked.

"Yes. Who's this?"

"It's Claire."

"Oh," she said.

I waited for her to speak again, but she obviously had no plans to.

"I'm calling about Shelly. I wanted to see how she's doing."

She hesitated for a second before speaking, "She's doing good. She asks about you a lot."

I closed my eyes, feeling guilty. With everything going on in my life, I hadn't thought about Shelly in weeks.

"Do you think I could see her? I know it would have to be when Rick isn't home. I can pick her up anytime."

"Claire—"

"Please, Tammy. I want to see her. Rick never has to know. I'm not asking for anything else, I swear. I just miss her."

She sighed. "Can you be here at one? That's when she gets home from summer school. Rick works until four now, so you'll have to make the visit short or keep her overnight."

I smiled even though she couldn't see me. "I'll be there. I want her to stay with me overnight. I'll make sure I get her to school on time tomorrow morning, but she'll need clothes and such. Can you pack an overnight bag for her? Also, make sure she brings her bathing suit."

"Yeah, I'll have everything ready. It's good to hear from you, Claire," she said before ending the call.

I shoved my phone in my pocket, still smiling over the fact that I was going to spend time with Shelly. I decided we were going to have a full-out slumber party tonight. I would make sure Shelly had the best night ever.

I looked in the pantry, noticing there wasn't a lot of food that a ten-year-old would want to eat. I definitely needed to run to the grocery store. I ran upstairs and grabbed my purse out of my room before heading back downstairs. As I came around the corner, I almost ran into Cooper.

"Whoa! What's the rush?" he asked.

"Sorry. I didn't mean to run into you. I have a friend coming over this afternoon, so I'm going to the grocery store. I'll be back later."

"Okay…" Cooper said, giving me a strange look.

I shrugged it off before grabbing my keys and opening the door leading to the garage. I hurried to my car and got inside. As soon as the garage door rose, I backed the car out and headed down the driveway.

The drive to the store only took a few minutes. After I grabbed a cart, I started walking up and down the grocery aisles, filling my cart with every bit of junk food I could think of. I loaded up on chips, soda, candy bars, candy, ice cream, whipped cream, chocolate fudge, Pop-Tarts, kid cereal, and a few other things I thought she would like. Once I was finished, I headed over to the electronics department and bought two movies I'd heard her mention before along with a couple of CDs I thought she would like. Next, I went to the toy aisle. Deciding what to get her was harder than I'd thought it would be. She wasn't a kid-kid anymore, but she wasn't a teenager either. I finally settled on a couple of dolls, a jewelry-making kit, and one of those dogs that was supposed to be lifelike.

I took everything to the cashier and paid with the card Robert had given me. I felt a small twinge of guilt over spending his money, but I quickly pushed it aside. He'd given me the card himself. It wasn't like I was stealing from him.

After everything was loaded into the car, I drove home. I carried in the food first, making sure to put the ice cream in the freezer so that it wouldn't melt. I brought in her presents next and took them to my old room. I laid everything out on the bed. I was excited to see her reaction when she saw her presents. Shelly was a good kid and deserved every single thing I'd bought her. I just hoped Rick wouldn't ask too many questions about where everything had come from.

I headed back out into the hallway. Just as I reached the top of the stairs, I noticed that Robert's bedroom door was open. When Cooper and another man stepped out, my eyes widened in surprise.

What the hell is Cooper doing in Robert's room?

Cooper looked up and saw me watching him. He froze, his face a mask of shock.

I started walking toward him and the other man, determined to figure out what was going on. "What were you doing in my room?" I demanded.

The man glanced at Cooper without speaking. Obviously, he wasn't going to tell me anything. I studied him, trying to figure out who he was. He was dressed in slacks and a button-down shirt. His hair was cut military short. His eyes were a piercing blue color. His arms were well defined, almost as muscular as Cooper's.

"Well?" I asked when neither of them spoke.

"I thought you weren't going to be home until later," Cooper said.

"Stop avoiding the question. What were you doing in there?"

Cooper frowned at me and held up a shirt. "I needed a dress shirt, so I borrowed one of Dad's. Chill out."

"You seriously expect me to believe that?" I asked, cautiously eyeing the shirt.

Cooper was lying to me, but I wasn't sure why.

"Yeah, I do, because it's the truth. Now, if you'll excuse us…" Cooper moved past me with his friend following him.

His friend looked back at me once, and I saw pity in his eyes before he disappeared into Cooper's room with Coop.

Pity?

I had no idea why he was looking at me like that. I shook my head as I turned and walked back down the stairs. They were keeping something from me.

I walked into the kitchen a few minutes later, and Ellie was standing at the sink, rinsing out a bowl.

"Hey, Ellie?"

"Hmm?" She turned to me.

"Who's Cooper's friend?"

"I'm not sure. He never gave his name. Why do you ask?"

I shrugged, not wanting her to know he had been in Robert's room with Cooper. "No reason. I was just curious."

"I've seen him here a couple of times, but I've never really talked to him. He's rather quiet, which is strange, considering the fact that he's friends with Cooper."

I laughed. "True story. Hey, can I ask you for a favor?"

"Anything, honey." She smiled at me.

"Can you make lasagna for dinner tonight? I have a friend coming over, and it's her favorite."

"Certainly. I'll have it ready around five."

"That's perfect. I'm going to go pick her up now. We'll grab something small for lunch and then head back. I'd love if you could join us tonight."

"I wish I could, but I have plans. Maybe next time." Ellie smiled at me.

"Sounds like a plan."

I waved good-bye before heading back out to the garage. A few minutes later, I was on my way to pick up Shelly. I couldn't keep the silly grin off my face over the thought of spending time with her. I'd really missed her. We'd gone from sharing a room to never seeing each other at all.

I pulled up in front of the house. Shelly and Tammy were standing on the front porch, obviously waiting for me. Shelly caught sight of me as I climbed out of my car. I laughed when I saw her jumping up and down. I barely made it to the porch before she tackled me in a hug so tight that I could barely breathe.

"I missed you, kiddo," I said as I hugged her back. I was so happy to see her again.

Once I managed to free myself, I looked up at Tammy. She was staring at my car in surprise.

"Hi, Tammy," I said politely.

Her eyes snapped to me. "Hi, Claire. It's good to see you again."

"You, too."

She glanced at the car again and then back at me. "That's a really nice car. It's much nicer than the one you owned when you left."

I shrugged. "It's my fiancé's car."

Her mouth dropped open in shock, but she said nothing.

Ha! You never thought I'd make it, and neither did Rick, but look at me now.

"Are you ready to go, kiddo?" I asked.

"Yep!" Shelly picked up her bag and slung it over her shoulder.

She waved good-bye to Tammy before following me to my car. She climbed into the passenger seat and tossed her bag down onto the floor as I walked around the front of the car before getting in.

"Wow. This is a really nice car, Claire."

"Thanks, Shelly."

"Can I ask you a question?"

"You already did, but go ahead," I teased.

"What's a fiancé?"

I laughed out loud. "It's a boyfriend who you promise to marry."

"Oh, okay. Now, I understand."

"Are you ready to have some fun? I thought we could stop and grab something to eat before we head home. My friend Ellie is making you something special for dinner, so we can't eat a bunch now, okay?"

"Sounds good to me," she said excitedly.

I drove to a fast-food restaurant, and I got her a kid's meal. We sat inside and talked as she ate her chicken nuggets. She told me about her friends in summer school and what she'd been up to in the past month. I was relieved to hear that things were still the same in Rick and Tammy's house. Rick had never been physically abusive, but that didn't mean he would never be that way. The thought of him laying a hand on Shelly or the other foster kids made my blood boil. If I ever found out he had, he'd be a dead man.

We continued to chat as she finished her meal. I grinned as she talked nonstop on the way back to the car and the entire drive home. Shelly obviously had a lot to catch me up on from the past few weeks. It made me happy to know that she wanted to tell me every little detail of her life. As a foster child, I knew that most of us were usually fairly tight-lipped about what we told people, both about our presents and our pasts. It was one of the few protections we could offer ourselves in a system where we had absolutely no control.

When I pulled up my driveway, Shelly's mouth dropped open. Her eyes stayed glued to the house until we drove into the garage.

"Claire, are you rich now?" she asked.

I smiled. "A little bit, yeah."

"Wow." She climbed out of the car.

She slowly followed me up to her temporary room, taking in every inch of the house that she could see.

"Come on, slowpoke. I have a surprise for you," I said as we walked down the hallway.

"What is it?" she asked excitedly.

"Open this door and find out."

I didn't need to tell her twice. She flung the door open and ran inside. She stopped short when she saw all the presents on the bed. With a squeal of delight, she dropped her bag to the floor and ran over to the bed.

She picked up the CDs first and clutched them to her chest. "Is this all for me?"

"Yep, all of it."

She squealed again as she dropped the CDs and then picked up the movies. "Can we watch these tonight?"

"We can do whatever you want," I told her.

The toys were hit and miss. She loved the jewelry maker and the dog, but she laughed at the dolls.

"I'm not five, Claire. Gesh," she teased.

"Well, *sorry*. I'll buy you a book and some clothes next time."

She turned toward me and stuck out her tongue. Then, her eyes fell on something behind me. "Who are you?" she asked.

I turned to see Cooper leaning against the doorframe. He seemed surprised to see that my *friend* was a kid, but he tried to hide it.

"I'm Cooper." He smiled at her.

It was probably the first genuine smile I'd ever seen from him. He had a nice smile when he wasn't using it with the forces of evil. It made him look younger and, well, happier.

"Is this your fiancé, Claire?" Shelly asked.

"My what?" I sputtered. "No, Cooper is just my…friend."

I looked back to see Cooper smirking at me, but he wisely kept his mouth shut.

"It's nice to meet you, Cooper. I'm Shelly. Claire and I shared a room before our foster dad kicked her out."

Cooper gave me a questioning look before smiling at Shelly. "Well, it's nice to meet you, Shelly."

"Claire, can we watch these movies now?" she asked.

"We can if you want, but I thought you might want to go swimming first," I told her.

"You have a pool, too? Wow, this house has everything." She glanced at Cooper. "Even cute boys."

Cooper laughed. "I knew I liked you, Shelly."

"All right, Cooper and I are going to leave you alone, so you can change into your suit. I need to change, too, so just open the door when you're ready, and I'll come back to get you." I walked to the door. I pushed Cooper out into the hallway before walking out myself.

"Okay!" Shelly said as I closed the door.

I ignored Cooper as I walked down the hall to my room. After closing the door, I walked to the dresser and pulled out a black bikini. After I changed, I grabbed two extra large towels out of the bathroom and headed back to Shelly's room. The door was open, and she was sitting on the bed when I poked my head inside.

"Ready?" I asked.

"Yep!" She jumped up and ran out the door.

I laughed as I hurried to keep up with her. I'd missed this little girl so much.

Shelly and I spent most of the afternoon in the pool. I knew she loved the water, but Rick had refused to buy her a pool every summer. I laughed as I watched her do handstands in the shallow end of the pool. Then, we raced a few times to see who could swim to the other side the fastest. She won almost every time.

After about an hour, I told her I was going to lie on one of the reclining chairs near the pool. She rolled her eyes at me, and then she continued to dog paddle away. I watched her for a minute before climbing out of the pool and walking to the recliner. I sat down on it and relaxed, enjoying the sun's warmth on my skin. I closed my eyes, but I kept my ears open in case Shelly needed me.

After a few minutes, I felt like someone was watching me. The hairs on my arms stood up, and I opened my eyes to see who it was. I jumped when I saw Cooper sitting in the chair next to me.

"What are you doing?" I asked.

"The same thing you are—sitting here," he said.

"Smart-ass. I meant, what are you doing out here with us? Don't you have someone else to terrorize?"

"Nah, I thought I'd come out here and annoy you."

"Goody," I mumbled before closing my eyes. Maybe if I pretended he wasn't around, he'd go away. It was doubtful, but I was willing to try.

"What you did for Shelly was really nice," Cooper said after a few minutes of silence.

I opened my eyes and looked at him again. "What do you mean?"

"Buying her that stuff, bringing her here to spend time with you. She obviously worships the ground you walk on, and I know it means a lot to her."

I looked over to see Shelly lying on her belly on a pool raft, watching Cooper and me.

"She's a special little girl."

"I can tell, and she obviously has good taste in men," he said.

I laughed, remembering her mentioning how cute he was. "She's only ten. She still thinks boys have cooties. She was only being nice."

"So, you don't agree with her?"

"Nope," I said, refusing to meet his eyes.

Cooper knew what he looked like. There was no way I was going to inflate his ego by admitting that I found him attractive.

"Liar." He hesitated for a moment. "Want to tell me why you were kicked out of your foster home?"

"I'm surprised it wasn't in Robert's file on me," I said, not bothering to hide my annoyance. "My foster dad, Rick, kicked me to the curb on my eighteenth birthday just because he didn't have to keep me any longer."

"That sucks," he said quietly.

"Yeah, it did. I had no clue how I was going to survive. During those first few days, there were times when I really doubted if I would."

"I'm sorry you went through that, Claire. You didn't deserve to be treated that way," he said.

I shrugged. "It doesn't matter. What's done is done. Besides, if he hadn't kicked me out, I never would've met Robert. I suppose I should thank Rick for kicking me out."

Cooper snorted. "Yeah, meeting my dad isn't what I'd call lucky, Claire."

"Why are you so hard on him, Cooper? He's done nothing but take care of me, and you know it."

He shook his head. "I'm not getting into this with you right now. Have fun with your friend, Claire."

I watched as he stood and walked away. He turned back right before he opened the door. "Claire?"

"Yeah?"

"I can't wait to hear how the party went last night."

Ah, there's the asshole I know and hate.

When it was time to eat, Shelly refused to get out of the pool, but I managed to get her inside. Once she took a bite of Ellie's lasagna, she stopped complaining. I laughed as I watched her eat as if she were starved.

We spent the evening curled up together in front of the TV, watching both movies I'd bought. She fell asleep on the couch, and I was forced to carry her upstairs. Thankfully, she was a tiny little thing, or I never would've made it.

Once she was tucked safely in bed, I kissed her forehead and walked to my own room. I set my alarm, so I could get up in time to get her to school the next morning. I hated that our time together was over, but I vowed to spend more time with her. As long as I picked her up when Rick wasn't around, I didn't see how it would be a problem.

The last thing I thought of before drifting off to sleep was that Robert had never called.

I dropped Shelly off at school the next morning, promising that I would spend time with her again soon. She started crying as she climbed out of my car, and I felt horrible. She obviously hated staying with Rick and Tammy, and I couldn't really blame her.

We decided to leave her new toys at my house. That way, she would have something to play with when she came to visit, and we wouldn't have to worry about Rick asking where they came from. I hated how we had to hide the fact that we were spending time together because of that asshole.

A thought occurred to me as I drove through Morgantown. Shelly was part of the foster system, and from what she'd told me, no one would claim her. Maybe if I talked to Robert, he would be willing to adopt her. My heart soared at the thought alone. She would be taken care of and loved, no matter what. I made a mental note to speak to him about it when he made it back from his trip.

When I got home, I changed into my bathing suit and walked down to the pool. I had no plans for the day besides working on my tan. I slathered on tanning oil before setting a timer and turning onto my stomach. I knew I would fall asleep, and I didn't want to burn to a crisp.

Sure enough, I woke up to the sound of the timer going off. I opened my eyes to reset it and rolled onto my back. I started to close my eyes again, but out of the corner of my eye, I caught Cooper walking over to me.

I groaned when he sat down next to me. "Really, Coop? You feel the need to visit me again?"

He grinned. "Coop? Damn, I think you must like me after all. No one calls me Coop but my friends and Ellie."

I rolled my eyes. "I've been hanging out with Ellie, and that's what she constantly calls you. It just slipped out."

"I'm sure it did. Where's Shelly?"

"I dropped her off at school this morning."

"School? It's summer."

"Rick doesn't like the younger kids hanging around the house all the time, so he makes them go to summer school. It's stupid, but Shelly likes it."

Cooper frowned. "It sounds like this Rick guy is a real ass."

"He is, but he'd never hurt Shelly or the other kids. If he ever did try anything, I can promise you that he wouldn't be walking around for long afterward."

We both stayed silent for a few minutes. I couldn't stop myself from glancing over at Cooper. He was shirtless, wearing only his swim trunks. My eyes roamed over his chest and stomach, taking in every dip and curve of his skin. I had the undying urge to run my hands over every inch of him to see if his skin was as soft as it looked.

I slammed my mental brakes, and I quickly looked away from him. He was Robert's *son*, for God's sake. He would be my stepson soon enough. I was a sick individual to even think of him that way. It didn't matter how good he looked. He was off-limits. I just wished my eyes and the rest of my body would realize that.

"So, how was the party?" Cooper asked.

"Ugh, I don't even want to talk about it," I said.

"Oh, come on. It couldn't have been that bad. What did you do? Fall asleep from boredom?"

"It definitely wasn't boring. I'll tell you that much."

"Care to elaborate? I've been to those *parties*. I'd rather jack off with a cactus in my hand than go to another one."

"Oh my God, Cooper!" I shouted, disturbed.

"What? It's the truth. Those parties are always a snorefest. Tell me what happened to make this one different."

"I was the center of attention. Some woman named Sandra pretty much told me I was a gold-digging whore in front of everyone. Well, she didn't say those words, but the message was still the same."

"Sandra Buckhannon? Shit, I haven't seen that woman in over a year. I never could stand her, but my mom liked her. She used to yell at me whenever I told her I thought Sandra was a bitch."

"For once, I agree with you on something. She was horrible to me. I've never been so embarrassed in my life."

My eyes welled up with tears as I thought about her hateful words. Cooper seemed to notice. He sat up and turned so that he was facing me. He had a look on his face that I didn't understand.

"Hey, don't cry. Sandra's a fuckin' piece of work. Don't pay any attention to what she says, okay? You're not a gold-digger, and you're definitely not a whore."

I snorted as I brushed my tears away. "What? You're defending me now? You think the same about me."

"No, actually, I don't. I did when I first met you, but after reading that damn file and talking to you, I know you're not. I'm sorry that I said those things to you that night we met. You didn't deserve to hear them."

I looked at him in surprise. For the first time ever, he was being nice to me. I couldn't help but wonder why. "Well, thanks for not thinking I'm a whore, I guess."

He laughed. "You're welcome. Stay here. I'm going to get us something to drink. You look like you need lots and lots of alcohol."

I watched him stand and leave, trying to figure out how he'd gone from a thank-you to getting us drinks. I shook my head. Cooper was one mystery I doubted I'd ever figure out.

A few minutes later, he returned with four beers.

I raised an eyebrow in surprise. "Thirsty?"

He grinned. "They're for both of us. I thought we could sit out here and get drunk."

"You can't be serious. It's not even noon, Cooper. Besides, I don't really drink. The spa place gave me these fruity drinks, and after two of them, I thought I was going to pass out."

"Lightweight," he teased. "Come on, drink with me. I'm bored."

"You drink when you're bored?" I asked.

He glanced down at my tiny bikini top. "Among other things."

I blushed and crossed my arms over my chest. "Good to know."

He laughed as he handed me a beer, forcing me to uncross my arms. I didn't miss the way his eyes flashed to my chest before looking back up to my face.

"Chill out, Stepmommy. You're always so serious. I think it's time you had some fun."

I took a sip of beer and frowned. "This tastes like ass."

He grinned. "Just keep drinking. The more you drink, the better it tastes."

I looked at the bottle in my hand. *What the hell? Let's get drunk.*

I wasn't drunk, but I was quickly getting there.

Cooper had kept encouraging me to drink the beer I was holding. As soon as my first one had disappeared, he'd shoved a new full bottle into my hand. After his first, he'd walked back inside and brought out a bottle of Jack Daniel's and a shot glass. I'd wrinkled my nose when he let me sniff the whiskey. It had smelled worse than my beer tasted.

Now on my third beer, I felt warm all over, and it wasn't because of the sun. I smiled as I stared up at the sky, watching the fluffy white clouds passing by. Cooper was right. I'd needed this. I was constantly strung so tight that it felt good to just relax and stop worrying. All the things that always weighed so heavily on my mind were now distant thoughts.

"What are you smiling about over there?" Cooper asked.

I glanced over at him before turning my attention back up to the sky. I noticed a cloud that looked like a bunny and laughed. "No reason really. I just feel happy for once."

"And you're not normally happy?"

I shrugged. "I am, but it seems like every time I start to relax, something happens. It's nice to just sit here and watch the clouds." I pointed up at the cloud shaped like a bunny. "Look, there's a bunny. See its little fluffy tail?"

He looked up. "All I see is a bunch of cotton balls."

I rolled my eyes. "You have to look, really look."

He sighed before looking skyward again. "Where?"

I pointed toward it again. "Right there. See it? It's upside down, but you can totally see its floppy ears, too."

He laughed at me. "Yeah, I kind of see it. You're a dork, Claire."

I stuck my tongue out at him. "Am not."

He grinned at me. "I rest my case."

I ignored him as I took another drink of my beer. I frowned when I noticed that it was almost empty. Cooper seemed to notice it as well. He grabbed the bottle out of my hand and put a full one in it. Apparently, he had a hidden beer stash somewhere on his person.

"Can I ask you something?" He stared at me.

"I guess." I took a sip.

"If you weren't with my dad, what would you be doing right now?"

"Why would you ask me that?"

"Just humor me."

Between his hypnotic gaze and the alcohol coursing through my blood, I decided to answer him. "I'd probably be at work."

"And what would you be doing if you weren't there?"

I shrugged. "I'd probably be at the library or the gym. I was staying there before Robert brought me here. The gym was a lot better than where I was staying before that."

"Where? Your foster house?" he asked.

I shook my head. "No, after they kicked me out, I lived in my car until my boss offered his office at the gym as a temporary bedroom."

When Cooper didn't respond, I looked over at him. The look of rage on his face made me freeze in shock.

"You slept in your car?" he asked.

"Well, yeah. It was there or nowhere. It's not a big deal."

"Yes, it is a big deal. Jesus, Claire. No wonder you're staying with my dad. If I had that to go back to, I'd hang around for as long as I could."

"I'm not staying here because of what I left behind, Cooper! I told you, I'm not like that!" I said angrily. *How dare he think that's the only reason I'm staying here!*

"That's not what I meant, Claire. I know you have seen a little bit of my father's real personality shining through every once in a while. I heard your fight with him over the fact that he quit your job for you. It's only going to get worse if you stay here. I wish you could see that."

"Cooper, just drop it. I don't want to talk about this with you. I want today to be fun," I said.

He jumped out of his chair and started pacing in front of me. My eyes widened in surprise when he stopped and kneeled down next to me. His face was inches from mine as he stared into my eyes. My body kicked into sexual overdrive with his nearness. I cursed my traitorous body as I tried to reel in my emotions before he could see them written plainly on my face. My body wanted him, and a small part of my mind did, too. He made me feel things I shouldn't be feeling. I tried to steady my breathing as I thought of anything besides the fact that he was inches from me. His full lips were inches from mine. All it would take was a couple of inches for me to kiss him.

"Why won't you protect yourself, Claire? You're staying with him because you think it's safe, but it's not." He closed his eyes for a brief moment before opening them again. "If you're worried about money, I can loan you enough to get the hell out of Morgantown. I want to help you. Please let me help you."

"I don't need your help, Cooper. Yes, Robert can be controlling, but he'd never hurt me."

"You're wrong, Claire. You're so wrong. Once you're his, it's over. There's nothing I can do to protect you. But right now? You can still run."

"I don't want to run, Cooper! Why can't you accept that?" I shouted.

"Because you deserve better!" He reached out and grabbed my upper arms firmly. "I saw what being with him did to my mom, and she was a hell of a lot stronger than you, Claire. You're innocent and sweet and everything that he doesn't deserve. When he's through with you, there will be nothing left of you! I refuse to watch that happen again!"

I opened my mouth to respond, but I was cut off when his lips found mine. He leaned closer until our bodies were flush against each other. I gasped in shock as he thrust his tongue into my mouth. I sat there in complete shock as he kissed me with enough passion to knock me senseless. I knew it was wrong, but I kissed him back. A voice in the back of my head screamed at me to stop, but I couldn't. Nothing in this world would stop me from kissing Cooper right now. It was everything my body was craving.

My hands found his hair, and I tugged on it gently, pulling him closer to me. His moan of pleasure made me smile against his lips. I shivered as his hands slid down my arms and stopped just above the top of my bikini bottom. He ran his thumbs across my hips, making me shudder. His touch felt like liquid fire, and I couldn't help but want to be burned.

Cooper's lips broke away from mine before kissing a trail up my jaw to my ear. He kissed the sensitive spot below my ear before continuing down to my neck. I threw my head back in ecstasy as his kisses made my blood run hot. I felt a throbbing between my legs, begging me for release. I tried to rub my legs together to ease the ache, but it was impossible with Cooper on top of me. All I managed to do was press my core tighter against his growing erection. His body was coiled tight with tension as he kissed the swell of my breasts and then pulled away. His breathing was as uneven as mine as he stared down at me.

"I've wanted to do that since the first time I saw you, Claire."

I said nothing as I stared at him in shock. Now that his lips weren't attacking me, a wave of horror overcame me. I couldn't believe what I'd just done. I'd kissed Robert's son.

Oh my God.

I shoved at him, trying to make him move. "Cooper, please let me up," I said desperately.

"No, not until you listen to me." He cupped my face. "I will protect you from my father. All you have to do is ask, Claire. I care about you, and I'll do anything to help you."

"Cooper, please!" I shoved him harder.

He sighed before standing. I scrambled to get off the recliner. Once I was upright, I headed for the door. Before I'd made it a foot, Cooper stopped me by wrapping his arms around my waist.

"Where do you think you're going?" he asked.

"I can't handle this, Cooper! I kissed you. Oh my God, I kissed you. You're going to be my *stepson*."

He laughed. "I don't care what you're supposed to be to me. All I know is that I want to keep you away from my father." He paused. "And I want you in my bed. You can't deny that you want it, too, Claire, especially not after you kissed me like that."

I struggled to free myself from his grip. Finally, he gave in and released me.

I spun to face him. "That will *never* happen again, Cooper. I'm not a whore."

"I never said you were!" Cooper shouted. "Why do you always go back to that?"

"Because we both know what you really think of me! I'm not stupid, Coop! You want me to sleep with you, so you can tell your dad, and he'll kick me out."

I didn't believe that, but I wanted to hurt him the only way I could—with words. The passion I'd felt as he kissed me wasn't faked. I knew that he wanted me, but that was a line that neither of us could cross.

He froze. "Is that what you think this is about? You think I'm that fucking low?" He shook his head, disgusted. "You know what? Fuck you, Claire. I'm out of here."

He stormed past me, not once glancing back at where I stood.

Tears ran down my cheeks. I hated that I'd hurt him, but I hadn't known what else to do. I wanted Cooper as much as he wanted me, and that could never happen. I'd never felt so ashamed in my life.

I had Robert, and I wanted Cooper. I was disgusting.

I opened my eyes slowly and glanced at the clock. It was just after three in the morning. Something had woken me up, but I wasn't sure what. I rolled over and closed my eyes, hoping that I would fall back asleep quickly.

After Cooper's sudden departure, I'd waited all day and into the evening for him to come home. I'd spent the day replaying what had happened between Cooper and me over and over in my head. I still couldn't believe that he'd kissed me or that I'd kissed him back. What we had done was wrong, but I couldn't stand the fact that Cooper might hate me for what I'd said. All I'd wanted was to make things right between us. Once he forgave me, I would stay far away from him and hope that whatever feelings I had for him would fade. I'd finally given up at midnight, accepting the fact that Cooper wasn't coming home.

Just as I was drifting off, I heard a sound coming from down the hall. I sat straight up in bed, my heart pounding. Robert was still out of town, and Cooper hadn't been home when I'd fallen asleep earlier. I heard what sounded like a moan. I threw off the covers and stood. If someone was in the house who wasn't supposed to be, I needed to know. I couldn't just hide in bed and hope that the person wouldn't find me.

I grabbed my phone off the nightstand and walked to the door. I opened it carefully so that it wouldn't make a sound, and I stepped out into the hall. Since it was pitch black, I felt my way along the hallway. I didn't want to alert anyone by turning on the hallway light. I heard something fall to the ground in either Cooper's room or one of the guest rooms. I walked quietly down the hall with my cell phone clutched tightly in my hand. I cursed myself for not bringing something else that I could use as a weapon if I needed it.

I reached my old room first and opened the door to glance inside. When no one jumped out and attacked me, I threw the door open and flipped on the lights, but I found nothing. After checking the closet, I walked back into the hallway. I froze when I heard a moan. It sounded like it was coming from Cooper's room.

I walked the last few feet and stopped outside his door. It wasn't closed completely. It stood open about an inch. Taking a deep breath to prepare myself for whatever I would find in Cooper's room, I pushed the door open a few more inches and peeked inside. What I saw stopped me dead in my tracks.

The lamp on Cooper's nightstand was on, revealing a completely naked woman lying on Cooper's bed. Her body convulsed as she moaned and gasped for air. I couldn't look away. Instead, my eyes drifted farther down the bed. Cooper lay half on and half off the bed with his head buried between her legs.

"Oh God, Coop, don't stop," the woman gasped.

I stood frozen in the doorway as I watched him pleasure her with his hand and mouth. My eyes traveled down Cooper's body as if they had a mind of their own. He was still wearing a pair of jeans, but his shirt was lying next to the bed. The muscles in his arms and back rippled as he drove his fingers into her over and over again.

My body responded to the scene before me. I was mortified to realize that I was quickly becoming aroused as I watched him. Heat pooled between my legs, and my nipples pushed against the thin silk nightgown I'd worn to bed. No man had ever done to me what Cooper was doing to this woman. I was ashamed to admit that neither of the men I'd ever been with—a boyfriend back in high school and Robert—had brought me the pleasure this woman was obviously experiencing.

"I'm coming. Fuck, Coop!" the woman moaned as she wrapped her legs around his neck and pulled him closer.

Her body arched off the bed, and she cried out, but Cooper never stopped his assault on her body. When she finally relaxed back onto the bed, he released her and stood. A small gasp escaped me as he reached for the button on his jeans and popped it open.

Cooper, apparently hearing me, turned to face me. Our eyes locked. His green eyes were wild with lust. He licked his still wet lips as his eyes traveled down my skimpy nightgown. When his eyes found mine again, the hunger had darkened them so that they looked black. Arousal shot through my body. Dear God, I wanted him, too.

I finally found the ability to move when he took a step toward me. I turned and ran. It was all I could do. I had to escape, or I'd do something that I'd later regret. I didn't stop at my bedroom. Instead,

I ran past it, down the stairs, and to the front door. I quickly disabled the security system and threw open the front door.

I dropped down onto the bottom step of the porch as I tried to remember how to breathe. The cool night air felt frigid against my overheated skin. After a few minutes, my breathing returned to normal, and the tingles between my legs finally dissipated. I rested my head on my knees, trying to process what I'd just seen.

Cooper had been having oral sex with another woman. Dear God, he was probably having actual sex with her right now. One thing I knew for sure, I couldn't go back into the house yet. There was no way I could listen to him having sex with someone else. And I would have to listen to it. The woman obviously wasn't going to be quiet, especially if she enjoyed the sex more than whatever he was doing when I saw them.

Arousal and sadness warred inside of me. I had no right to feel either, but I did, especially after this afternoon. I shouldn't care about what he was doing with another woman right now. I'd made my bed, and now, I had to lay in it. I was with Robert, and I knew I'd never leave him. Having these kinds of feelings about his son was wrong. It was sick. I was fucked-up in the head, no question about it.

What woman lusts after her fiancé's son?

I closed my eyes, trying to block thoughts of Cooper from my mind. I had to get past this attraction for him. That was the only answer.

I sat outside for what felt like at least an hour before silently slipping back through the front door. I activated the security system before climbing the stairs. Standing at the top of the staircase, I strained my ears, trying to make out any sounds coming from Cooper's room. If I heard so much as a whimper, I would run back outside.

After hearing nothing for a few minutes, I walked back to my room and closed the door. I grabbed my fuzzy robe off the hanger on the back of the door and shoved it against the crack underneath. Hopefully, it would keep me from hearing anything else tonight.

I crawled back into bed and pulled the blankets up to my chin. As I'd expected, sleep didn't come for the rest of the night.

I stayed in my room until well after noon the next day. I was terrified that I'd see Cooper, and after last night, I couldn't handle that. I wasn't sure that I'd ever be able to look at him again after what I'd witnessed.

I cursed myself at the surge of jealousy shooting through my body as I thought about him with that woman. Jealousy wasn't something I was accustomed to. All my life, I'd accepted that I couldn't have the things I wanted. I'd never felt any anger toward people who had what I wanted. But the burning hate I felt for the woman in Cooper's room last night wouldn't dissipate.

I couldn't help but wonder who she was. After Cooper's little scene out by the pool, I doubted that she was his girlfriend. If she were, he obviously wasn't very loyal to her. Maybe she was a random stranger or a fuck buddy. I began to feel annoyed with myself because I was really taking the time to try to figure out who this woman was. I forced myself to let the subject drop even though I knew it would nag at me until I found out.

I jumped when my phone started ringing on the nightstand. I walked over to it, and guilt washed over me when I saw Robert's name flashing across the screen. I answered quickly, not wanting to let my mind touch on the fact that this was the first time he'd called me since he left.

"Hello?"

"Claire, it's so good to hear your voice," Robert said.

"It's good to hear yours, too. I was starting to wonder if you'd forgotten about me."

"I'm sorry that I haven't called. I've been busy trying to get this mess taken care of. I was going to call you last night, but it was after midnight by the time I made it back to my hotel room."

"It's okay," I said. I refused to make Robert feel guilty over not calling me, especially after what I'd done behind his back. "Are you coming home soon?"

I hoped that he was. With Robert around, it would be much easier to avoid Cooper. He wouldn't try anything with his father in the same house—or maybe he would. My heart stopped as I wondered whether or not Cooper would tell his father that he'd kissed me and then caught me spying on him while he was practically having sex. Robert would kick me out faster than I could blink. I absolutely did not want to talk to Cooper, but I knew I would have to suck it up and pretty much beg him not to tell Robert what I'd done.

"In a couple of days, I promise. I also have one of my colleagues working on that case I mentioned to you before. He's doing very well with it and taking care of a lot of my work. Once I get back, we'll prepare to go to court. With the case he has built, I don't think we'll have any trouble winning."

"That's awesome, Robert," I said.

"It is. I'll be glad when this case is over, and everything is taken care of up here. Once I'm free, we'll be able to spend more time together."

"I can't wait."

I heard someone call his name in the background. It sounded like a woman's voice. I raised an eyebrow, wondering who he was with.

"I have to go, Claire, but I'll talk to you soon."

The line disconnected before I had a chance to reply.

I took a deep breath before knocking on Cooper's door. I knew he was inside. I could hear Seether's "Words as Weapons" blaring through the wall. When he didn't answer the door, I knocked louder. A second later, the music was cut off abruptly. Cooper opened the door and coolly stared at me.

"Can I help you with something?" he asked. His eyes were as cold as his tone.

I couldn't help but shiver. Cooper definitely knew how to get his point across.

"We need to talk." I pushed past him into his bedroom.

I glanced around, making sure to avoid looking at his bed. His room was different from what I'd expected. It was tidy, and not a single thing was out of place. He had a large bookcase against the far wall. Every shelf was filled with books. His computer desk sat next to it with a stack of textbooks piled neatly next to the keyboard. I glanced at their spines—chemistry, physics, and advanced calculus. That told me that Cooper was smart, and he was probably premed. His walls were bare. I was surprised not to see a single photo or poster. His room, one I assumed he'd had for years, looked like a guest room.

Cooper closed his bedroom door and turned to me. "What do you want to talk about?"

I didn't miss the smirk that he gave me. He obviously thought I wanted to talk about what I'd seen last night.

"I came to apologize for what I said yesterday. I was angry, and what I said wasn't true. I know you're not out to hurt me."

"Well, I'm glad that's cleared up," he said, sarcasm dripping from his voice. "Is that all you wanted?"

"No, it's not." I took a deep breath. "What happened yesterday shouldn't have happened. We both know that. I want you to promise me that you won't tell Robert. It would destroy us."

He laughed. "You really think my dad would care about that? I can promise you that he wouldn't. As long as you're here, hanging on his every word like a good little girl, he'll be happy. But if it makes you feel better, I won't tell him what happened by the pool."

My shoulders sagged in relief. "Thank you. Whether you think he would care or not, I know he would. I don't want him to hate me."

"I also won't tell him about last night," Cooper said, obviously ignoring my thank-you.

I tensed up. "Cooper…"

He grinned as he took a step closer to me. "I won't tell him about the look on your face as you watched me with another woman. I won't tell him about the lust in your eyes."

"I have no idea what you're talking about," I whispered as I took a step back.

My back hit the wall, but he continued to step closer. He stopped right in front of me and rested his hands on the wall next to my head so that he was caging me in.

"You're a terrible liar, Claire. Even now, you want me. Your pupils are dilated, and your breathing is uneven. You know what I can do, and you want it. You want to be the one on my bed with my head buried between your legs." He leaned closer so that his lips touched my ear. "All you have to do is ask. I promise, you'll be screaming when I'm done with you."

"You're seeing things that aren't there," I said breathlessly.

I hated how much I wanted the man in front of me. I'd never wanted someone the way I wanted him. I'd known that I was attracted to Cooper before Robert left, but I'd been able to control it. With Robert gone, Cooper was no longer pretending not to notice that I was interested in him. He knew, and he was doing everything he could to make me fall from grace. God, I wanted to.

He chuckled as he lowered one of his hands and cupped my breast. I sucked in a shocked breath as he ran his thumb over my nipple. In my thin cotton shirt and bra, I knew it was visible.

"Your body is telling me a different story. I bet if I slid my hand into those tiny shorts of yours, I'd find you drenched, wouldn't I?" He released my breast and slid his hand down my stomach. He continued down until he was cupping my throbbing center through my shorts. "You're hot for me, Claire. No matter what you say, I know the truth. The question is, what are you going to do about it?"

I stared into his green eyes. They were full of lust and uncontrollable need. I knew if I told him yes, he'd have me on his bed in less than a second.

His thumb pressed on my core, and I sucked in a sharp breath as pleasure spread throughout my body. It begged me to say yes even though I knew it would destroy everything I had with Robert. Having a moment of pleasure with Cooper would be more than Robert had given me. It would be everything.

I shoved Cooper's hand away before pushing him away and darting for the door. I threw it open and turned back to look at him. He hadn't moved. He still had one hand pressed against the wall with his back to me. Finally, he turned his head so that our eyes met. I took one look at him before I turned and ran.

When it came to Cooper, it seemed like all I could do was run.

I avoided the house for the rest of the day. Instead, I drove aimlessly around Morgantown as I tried to calm down. Cooper had more power over me than I'd realized. I had hated him at first, but after he'd shown me the kinder side of him, I'd realized that I did like him. Cooper was one of the most complex people I'd ever met. I felt like I saw a different side of him every time I peeled a layer of him away. Arrogant Cooper, secretive Cooper, kind Cooper, erotic Cooper—they all made him what he was. The more I knew about him, the more drawn to him I felt.

By the time I made it back to the house that evening, I'd made a solid plan. I would avoid being alone with Cooper at all costs. I didn't care if that meant staying away from the house until Robert came home. I would do whatever it took to keep him out of my head. I refused to be *that* woman—the whore, the cheater. I wouldn't be the woman his friends thought I was. Robert wasn't perfect, but that didn't make it okay for me to fuck around on him behind his back.

The house was quiet as I walked up the stairs and turned toward my room. Just as I reached my door, I caught movement out of the corner of my eye. I stopped and glanced back to see Cooper's door opening. The man I'd seen with Cooper before stepped out into the hallway. He headed for the stairs, but he froze when he saw me.

For some reason, I felt the need to talk to this man. I let go of the doorknob and started walking toward him. He stayed where he was as I reached him. I looked up at him, studying him. His eyes held the same pity from last time as he watched me.

"Who are you?" I finally asked, breaking the silence.

He looked away, refusing to answer me.

I sighed. "I don't know what it is about you, but I know you're not just Cooper's friend. Since he refuses to tell me, why don't you?"

He finally looked back to me. "I'm just his friend."

"Bullshit," I said. "Tell me the truth."

"Claire? What are you doing?" Cooper stepped out of his bedroom.

I looked up to see him approaching us, but his eyes were glued to his *friend*.

"I'm just talking to your friend, Coop. Is that a problem?"

"I should be going." The man started walking down the stairs.

I glared at his back until he disappeared out the front door. Once he was gone, I turned to Cooper.

"What are you up to?" I demanded.

"Why do you always think I'm up to something? I had a friend over. Is that not allowed, Stepmother?"

I winced at the title, and he smirked. He was back to being arrogant Cooper.

"You know what? Never mind." I turned and stormed down the hall to my bedroom.

"Claire?" Cooper called.

"What?" I nearly shouted. I was so aggravated with him.

"Your ass looks amazing in those shorts."

I slammed the door.

I woke up a few hours later, gasping for breath. I covered my eyes with my arm, willing my body to calm down. Even in sleep, Cooper had still found a way into my mind. His hands had caressed my body until I begged for more.

I'd never had a dream like that before. It had felt so real. Even after waking, my body was still humming with need and craving release. I hated that Cooper was in my head. I hated that I wanted him. I hated how he made me feel.

I sighed in defeat. No matter how determined I was to stay away from him, he was always there, right on the edge of my mind. My decision to avoid him was for the best. Robert said he wouldn't be home for a few more days. That gave me time to get a grip on my raging hormones. As long as I avoided Cooper, I would be okay.

The dream though was a problem. I shivered as I remembered the way his lips had felt on my skin, both in the dream and in real life. His kisses were hypnotic. They drove all rational thought from my mind. They were like a drug, and I was a junkie, desperately craving my fix.

Before I realized what I was doing, my hand slid down my flat stomach to the top of my sleep shorts. My fingers slipped inside and went down to where my body was still throbbing with need. I closed my eyes as I flicked my clit. I felt myself blush as I continued to rub. I'd never done anything like this, and I felt ashamed for a moment before my need took over.

A picture of Cooper—shirtless with only a pair of jeans—flashed through my mind. My eyes trailed over his body, taking in his strong arms, solid chest, and tight abs. In my mind, I ran my hands over every bump and crevice of his hard muscles. His soft groans of pleasure only spurred me on. My fingers moved faster, and my back arched off the bed. I pictured running my hand across the top of his shorts before hooking my fingers inside. I slowly pulled them down, inch by inch.

Before I could discover what was hidden, I came—hard. I cried out as stars exploded in front of my eyes. The feeling of pure pleasure was nothing like I'd expected. When I drifted back down into the known world, I realized that I'd just given myself my first orgasm—with Cooper's help.

Dear God, I was fucked.

The next morning, I awoke to the sound of someone knocking on my door. I climbed out of bed and stumbled over to the door. I opened it, assuming that Ellie needed something. I was surprised when I saw Cooper standing there.

"Coop? What do you want?" I was suddenly conscious of the fact that I hadn't brushed my hair or teeth. I probably looked like a wicked witch.

His eyes trailed down my body, stopping on my chest for a few seconds before continuing their descent. I crossed my arms over my chest, conscious of the fact that I wasn't wearing a bra.

When his eyes found mine again, he smiled. "I didn't mean to wake you up. I wanted to talk."

"About what?" I asked.

He held up two envelopes. "Can I come inside, please?"

I nodded as I stepped back. "This had better be good. I'm missing sleep for this."

I left the door open before heading to where he was sitting on my bed. I blushed as I remembered what I'd done on that bed only a few hours before. If he noticed the color in my cheeks, he didn't comment.

"Sit down. I have a lot to explain, and I'm sure it's going to shock you."

I sat down, making sure to keep a few inches between us. "Okay…"

"You asked who my friend was. His name is Jason. He's been working for me for a while."

"Wait—he works for you?" I asked, confused.

"He's a private investigator. I hired him a few months before my mom died."

"Why would you hire a private investigator?"

"Because I don't trust my dad."

I raised an eyebrow. "You had your dad investigated? Why?"

"Because he's an asshole, and I thought he was fucking around on my mom, but I needed proof."

He held up one of the envelopes, so I could take it from him.

"And I got it."

"Your dad was cheating?" I asked. It felt like the air in the room had been vacuumed out.

"Yes. Look in the envelope."

I opened it and pulled out several photos. All of them had Robert with women I didn't recognize. I counted three different women in the photos. In each one, Robert was holding, kissing, and touching the women in ways that made it very clear what had happened next.

I looked up at Cooper. "Why are you showing these to me?"

"Because you need to know." He handed me the other envelope. "Those were all before my mother died. These were after."

I opened the other envelope and pulled out more photos. I sucked in a shocked breath when I saw the first photo. "Sandra?"

He nodded. "Yeah, Brad's wife. I wasn't surprised when you told me she attacked you at the party. She wasn't doing it because of my mom though. She was doing it because she'd slept with him and thought he was going to marry her. From what Jason told me, my father promised her that they'd be together."

I flipped through the pictures. Most of them were photos of Robert with Sandra, but there was another woman as well. She was in the first set of pictures, too. All the photos had dates on them, and I noticed the last one had been taken a week before I met Robert.

"I can't believe he cheated on your mom. I'm so sorry, Cooper."

He shrugged. "It's what he does. He's always been an asshole, and my mom knew it. The night she died, I'd called her and asked her to come home. Dad was out of town, and I wanted to show her what Jason had found out for me." He swallowed hard. "I was going to tell her everything, but she never made it home."

The pain he felt was a living, breathing thing. Even I could feel it.

Without thinking, I dropped the pictures and pulled him to me. I hugged him tightly. "I'm so sorry, Cooper. I can't even imagine," I whispered.

"She died, not knowing what he was doing to her. If I'd shown her everything the day before when Jason brought them to me, she would've known. Maybe she wouldn't have gone to Sandra's house that night for dinner. Maybe she would've stayed home. If I'd told her, maybe she'd still be alive."

"You can't think like that, Cooper. Your mother's death wasn't your fault." I pulled away.

He shrugged again, clearly not wanting to talk about it. "I have a few more pictures I want to show you."

He pulled a small envelope out of his back pocket and handed it to me. "These were taken this week. Jason was here last night to drop them off."

My heart was beating a mile a minute as I slowly opened the envelope. Inside were photos of Robert with the woman I'd seen in both of the other envelopes. Instead of kissing or touching each other as they had in the others, they were sitting in a restaurant, having dinner. Another photo showed them hugging. There were a few more, but none of the photos showed Robert doing anything that flat-out proved he was cheating on me.

"Either he knows he's being followed, or his affair with that woman is over," Cooper said quietly. "Regardless, he's been photographed with her numerous times before, and he's with her again...instead of being home with you."

"Maybe he really isn't cheating." I stared at the photo of Robert and the mystery woman walking out of the restaurant.

She was beautiful with dark brown hair and dark eyes. She was slim but tall, much taller than I was. She screamed class while I felt like what I really was—a broken little girl who would never fit into Robert's world.

Cooper snorted. "Doubtful. Dad does whatever the fuck he pleases."

"Why did you show me these if they don't prove anything?" I asked.

"Because you deserve to know what kind of man he is, Claire." Cooper reached up and cupped my face. "You're so damn innocent. You have no idea what you're getting into with him. I've tried to warn you, but you wouldn't listen. I knew I needed proof."

"This doesn't prove anything, Cooper. Yes, he cheated on Marie, but that doesn't mean he's cheated or will cheat on me."

He shook his head. "You're so blind, Claire."

I watched as he gathered up the photos and shoved them in the envelopes. "I trust that you won't say anything to him."

"Of course I won't," I said. I wouldn't betray Cooper like that. "Cooper?"

"Yeah?"

"Why do you live here if you hate him so much?"

He looked uneasy. "Mainly because I can't touch the trust fund my mother set up for me until I'm twenty-one. Until then, I'm at *his* mercy. My mother was smart though, and she knew my father and I would never get along, so she set up the trust fund in her name, so he couldn't touch it."

I nodded. "That makes sense. Can I ask you something else?"

"Sure," he said, looking annoyed.

"Why are you still having him followed?"

He paused before shaking his head. "It doesn't matter."

I called his name as he walked out of the room, but he ignored me.

Whatever Cooper was trying to find out about his dad, he obviously hadn't managed to do it yet. If he had, Jason wouldn't still be hanging around.

I had a feeling that this was just the tip of the iceberg when it came to secrets. The Evans men seemed to be full of them.

Two days had gone by without a word from Cooper. I hadn't even been sure if he was staying at the house. Ellie had even noticed his absence and asked me what was going on. I'd shrugged, pretending that I knew nothing.

Robert had called me to let me know that things were going well in Pittsburgh. I'd almost asked him about the woman in the photos, but I couldn't bring myself to do it. If I asked him, he'd demand to know how I knew. I couldn't ask him without outing Cooper. I had no reason to feel any loyalty to him, but I did. He'd shown me those photos in an attempt to help me. I wouldn't use them against him. Whatever he was trying to catch Robert doing, he obviously hadn't found the proof he needed.

Three days after Cooper had shown me the photos, I was climbing into my car to pick up Shelly, and one of the other garage doors opened. Cooper pulled in next to me and shut off his car. He climbed out of his car, his eyes never leaving mine.

I gave him a weak smile before starting the car and pushing the button to raise the garage door. I jumped when he tapped on my passenger-side window. I pushed the button to lower it.

"Where are you going?" he asked.

"To pick up Shelly. I'm taking her to the zoo."

He reached through the open window and unlocked the door. I raised an eyebrow as he opened the door and climbed in next to me.

"What are you doing, Cooper?" I asked.

"I could use a trip to the zoo, too." He grinned at me.

"Really? I thought you'd have better things to do—like that chick." The last words had slipped out before I could stop myself. I closed my eyes, cursing myself for saying that.

"Jealous?" He smirked at me.

"Nope," I lied. "I just figured you'd rather spend time with your girlfriend instead of your soon-to-be stepmom and a little girl."

"So, you're jealous and fishing." He grinned. "Wendy isn't my girlfriend. She's just a friend."

I gave him a puzzled look. "I'm not exactly the best person when it comes to making friends, but I didn't think you did *that* with your friends."

"What? Have sex? You can say it, Claire. S-e-x. See? It's even easy to spell. And I suppose you're right. Wendy and I have a...mutual agreement. We're friends, but we also entertain each other when one of us calls the other."

"You're an ass. Get out of my car, so I can go get Shelly." I was disgusted and relieved at his explanation of Wendy. It was gross that he used her like that, but at the same time, it meant he wasn't with her. The green monster inside me simmered down.

"Don't get all pissy, Claire. I only called her because you decided to run from me."

I shook my head. "Get out, Cooper. I'm done talking about this."

"Nope. I want to see Shelly again. She's a cute kid."

"No, you just want to annoy me. I don't feel like dealing with you today, so please just get out of the car."

"I'll be on my best behavior. I promise."

I rolled my eyes as I threw the car in reverse and backed out of the garage. "So help me, if you're an ass, I will leave you there."

He laughed but said nothing. Instead, he turned on the radio and flipped the channels until he found the station he wanted. He looked over at me. "Is this okay?"

I nodded as Theory of a Deadman's "Drown" played. "Yeah, it's fine."

Neither of us spoke as I drove toward Shelly's. Instead, he started singing along with the song. I was surprised at just how good he was. When "Drown" ended, Angels Fall's "Drunk Enough" started playing. I hummed softly as Cooper sang every single word. I glanced over to see him watching me as he sang.

"You're really good," I blurted out, hoping to break the tension that filled the car.

He shrugged. "I like to sing, but I'd never want to do it professionally."

"I wish I could sing. I sound like a dying goat when I try."

He laughed as we pulled up to Shelly's house. She was standing on the porch, but as soon as she saw us, she waved and ran to the car. I unlocked the door so that she could climb in. She seemed surprised to see Cooper sitting in the front, but she quickly hid it as she settled into the backseat.

As soon as she was buckled up, I pulled away from the curb. I was taking her to a zoo that was less than an hour away. It wasn't as big as the one in Pittsburgh, but I knew she'd love it anyway. I'd been there once on a school field trip, but as far as I knew, Shelly had never been to a zoo before.

"Will you tell me where we're going now?" Shelly asked.

I grinned. "Nope. You'll just have to wait and see."

"Oh, man, this isn't fair," she whined.

Cooper turned around to look at her. "You'll love it. I promise."

She grinned, her cheeks filling with color. I wondered if that was what I looked like when Cooper was around.

"Hi, Cooper. I didn't know you were coming, too."

I'd never heard her talk so shyly. Even when I'd first met her, she'd been bursting at the seams to talk. I couldn't help but grin when I realized she had a crush on Cooper.

"I thought I'd tag along, so I could hang out with you again," he said.

I giggled at the way Shelly lit up at his words, earning me a glower from Shelly and a chuckle from Cooper. He obviously realized that Shelly was crushing on him, too.

Shelly chatted about a few of her friends as I drove to the zoo. With her in the car, I found myself relaxing. I was safe with Cooper as long as she was around.

When we reached the turnoff, she saw the sign for the zoo, and she squealed. "We're going to a zoo? I didn't even know one was this close!"

"Surprise!" I said as I navigated down the narrow two-lane road. "It's not big like the one in Pittsburgh, but they have tigers and even a giraffe. I know how much you like animals, so I thought it would be fun."

"This is so awesome! Do you think they'll have elephants, too?" she asked.

I shook my head. "No, I don't think they do. Sorry."

She shrugged. "It's okay. I'll settle for a giraffe."

Cooper glanced at me as we pulled into the parking lot. I parked the car, and Shelly began climbing out of the car.

"A giraffe is settling?" he asked.

"It is to a ten-year-old," I said as I opened my door and climbed out as well.

I met Shelly and Cooper at the front of the car.

Shelly grabbed both of our hands and started dragging us toward the ticket booth. "Come on, hurry up!"

I laughed as I let her pull me along. Shelly was always so happy. I couldn't help but smile when I was around her. She'd had a hard life, but it never seemed to bother her.

Cooper paid for our tickets even though I tried to stop him. He rolled his eyes at my protests as he handed his card over. Shelly was too busy staring at the tiny monkeys behind the glass to pay attention to either of us. Once Cooper paid, we walked over to where she was standing. I watched the monkeys as they chased each other around their enclosure.

"They're so cute!" Shelly said as she pressed her nose against the glass.

"Come on, let's go find some tigers." I pulled her away from the glass.

I was surprised when she kept her hand in mine as we walked through the zoo. We followed the path to where the tigers were caged. Cooper walked on the other side of Shelly, and she took his hand, too. He seemed as surprised as I was, but he tried to hide it. I wondered if Cooper had ever been around younger kids before. Everything Shelly did seemed to surprise him.

When we reached the tigers, Shelly let go of us and ran to their fence. She got as close as she could as she stared inside. The tigers paid absolutely no attention to us as they lay on the opposite side of the pen in the shade.

"Look at that one, Claire. It's white." Shelly pointed at the one farthest away from us.

There were three tigers total. I couldn't help but feel sorry for them. Their cage was large, but still, I couldn't imagine being caged up in such a small space for my entire life. Out in the wild, they would have had miles upon miles of space to roam and hunt.

"Why are you frowning?" Cooper asked quietly so that Shelly couldn't hear.

"I was thinking about how awful it is to be cooped up like that in a cage, unable to roam around."

"But they don't have to hunt or worry about surviving. They're safe here."

"I know but still."

"I guess I see where you're coming from. Just because you're safe and have everything you need doesn't mean you're happy."

I glanced over at him, wondering if we were still talking about the tigers. The hidden meaning in his words wasn't lost on me.

He looked away and turned his attention back to Shelly. "She's a good kid."

"She is. I've never seen someone as happy as her. She's grown up in the system, so I know her life hasn't been the greatest, but you'd never know it."

Cooper looked back at me. "Some people are stronger than others. I think Shelly's a fighter. No matter what happens, I think she'll be okay."

We spent the rest of the afternoon going from pen to pen, watching the animals as they played—or in most cases, lay in the shade. Several of them were asleep even, but Shelly didn't seem to mind. The zoo had a lot more animals than I remembered. They had chimpanzees, bears, lions, tigers, wild boars, spider monkeys, lemurs, leopards, goats, snakes, bobcats, camels, and even a donkey.

When we reached the giraffe enclosure, I laughed as Shelly tried to bribe the giraffe with food so that it would come over to us. It finally did, and I couldn't help but giggle as she squealed when it lowered its head and ate the food from her hand. Cooper pulled out his phone and snapped a few pictures as she petted the giraffe. When it finally lost interest in her, the giraffe headed over to a new group of people.

Cooper threw his arm around her shoulders and herded her toward the gift shop. I hung back as I watched the two of them together. Shelly hung on Cooper's every word, her eyes lighting up as she listened to him. The poor girl had it bad, but I couldn't really blame her. Cooper was so good with her. I wasn't sure what to think about that. There were so many sides to him, but my favorite was the way he acted around Shelly. He listened to everything she said, and he made the effort to truly spend time with her. I doubted if many adults had done that for her. Very few of my foster parents had paid much attention to me.

We left the gift shop with two stuffed bears—one for Shelly and one for me, courtesy of Cooper's credit card.

We decided to stop at a local diner for dinner before dropping Shelly off at her house.

I'd never been to the diner, but Cooper swore they had the best hamburgers around. That was all it took to convince Shelly that was where she wanted to eat. Apparently, Cooper's word was gold.

Shelly fell asleep only a few minutes after we climbed into the car. While driving to the diner, I glanced at her in the rearview mirror as she slept peacefully. I felt my heart being ripped apart as I thought about the fact that I'd have to take her home soon. I didn't want to. I wanted to pack all her belongings and bring her home with Cooper and me.

"Turn left here and then take a right into the parking lot," Cooper said, pulling me away from my thoughts.

I did as he'd said and parked the car in front of a bright yellow building. I gave him a skeptical look.

"What?" he asked.

"Yellow? Really?"

He shrugged. "I don't care if it's shit brown. Their food is to die for."

I rolled my eyes. I climbed out of the car and opened the back door. I gently shook Shelly to wake her up.

Her eyes sprang open, and she looked around. "I wasn't asleep. I was just resting my eyes," she said quickly.

Cooper laughed from behind me. "We know, kid. Everyone has to rest their eyes once in a while."

I grinned at him as Shelly climbed out of the car. I watched as she took Cooper's hand and led us to the diner's front door. I let out a tiny laugh. Obviously, Shelly didn't need me as long as Cooper was around.

A waitress seated us and took our drink orders before leaving us alone. Shelly had literally pulled Cooper down in the booth beside her. I hid my grin with my menu, pretending not to notice how much she liked him. Cooper gave me a look that told me he knew exactly what I was laughing over.

"Do I have to order off the kids menu?" Shelly asked.

I shook my head. "No, you can get whatever you want."

Her eyes lit up.

"Actual food. If you're still hungry after that, we can get dessert," I added.

She fist-pumped. "Yes! They have brownies here—*with ice cream.*"

She seemed to think that was the most marvelous thing since running water.

"You can have it after you eat actual food, missy," I said, pretending to act stern.

"You're no fun, Claire. You act like a mom. I bet Cooper would let me have nothing but ice cream and brownies if you weren't here."

I expectantly raised an eyebrow at Cooper.

He looked back and forth between Shelly and me, obviously trying to decide which side to take. "Claire's right, Shell. You gotta eat."

"Whatever," she grumbled as she flipped to the front of the menu. Her eyes lit up again. It didn't take much to excite this kid. "They have corn dogs! Can I have those?"

I nodded. "Go wild."

When the waitress came back with our drinks, she took our orders. Shelly made sure to say that she'd need brownies and ice cream once her food was finished. The waitress glanced at me to make sure. I nodded, and she wrote Shelly's order down.

Shelly kept Cooper busy as we waited for our food. I watched them as Shelly told him one story after another. Her face was so open. She trusted Coop completely. It made me wonder if I should trust him, too. I pushed the thought aside as the waitress put our plates down in front of us.

I dug into my burger, moaning in pleasure as I took my first bite. "Oh my gosh, this is the best burger ever."

Cooper grinned. "I gathered that from the way you were moaning."

I blushed before taking another bite. Once it was gone, I stuck my tongue out at him. "Shut up."

"That's a bad word," Shelly scolded me.

I stuck out my tongue at her, too. "Sorry."

Once our food was gone, the waitress brought out Shelly's brownies and ice cream. I smiled when I noticed that the waitress had put half an extra scoop in the bowl. She winked at me before dropping our bill on the table and walking away.

I watched in amusement as Shelly shoveled ice cream and brownies into her mouth. She was such a tiny thing. I had no clue where she was going to put it all.

"This is, like, the best thing ever! You guys have to try it!" Shelly said between mouthfuls.

"I'm good. Besides, I wouldn't want to take any of it from you," I teased.

She rolled her eyes. "Come on, Coop. Try it."

He grinned at her as he picked up a spoon and dug in. Shelly seemed just as excited over the fact that he was eating her ice cream as she was over actually having it.

"Isn't it good?" she asked him.

He nodded. "Not too bad." He looked up at me. "Try some, Claire."

I shook my head. "I'm good, really. After that burger, there's no way I could eat anything else. I'll explode."

"Come on. *Please*," Shelly said.

Cooper scooped another spoonful and held it up. "Try it, Claire." The tone of his voice deepened.

My eyes widened in surprise as he leaned forward so that the spoon was right in front of me.

"Open up for me."

I parted my lips, and he slipped the spoon inside my mouth. The taste of the rich chocolate and creamy ice cream barely registered as I stared at Cooper. His eyes were glued to my mouth as he slowly pulled the spoon away. The hunger in his eyes caused my body to tense. His eyes found mine as he licked his own lips, and I shuddered.

"See? I told you it was good," Shelly said.

My eyes never left Cooper's. "Yeah, it was."

After we left the diner, I dropped Shelly off. Rick was out of town, so we didn't have to worry about him catching me around. I kissed her forehead before watching her walk back to her house. I couldn't help but smile at how slow she was walking. I had no doubt that she'd crash as soon as she made it to her room.

"Thank you for being so good to her today," I told Cooper as I drove back to our house.

"What do you mean?"

"You actually made an effort to spend one on one time with her. That meant more to her than you realize."

"She's a good kid. It's impossible not to like her. It's too bad that we have to give her back."

I smiled. "Yeah, it is. Maybe one day I won't have to. I've thought about asking Robert to see how hard it would be to adopt her. I'm sure he'd be okay with it."

"*No.*"

I nearly pulled something in my neck as I looked over at him. The anger in his tone surprised me.

"What? Why?"

"I don't want her around my dad. He can barely stand to speak to me, and I'm his own blood. I can't imagine how he'd be with her. You're not bringing her into a household as fucked-up as ours."

I bit my lip to keep from telling him to fuck off.

He obviously noticed because he sighed. "I'm sorry. I didn't mean to sound like an ass. Look, we had a nice day. Let's try not to fight before we make it back to the house, okay?"

I nodded, but I refused to speak for the rest of the drive. Cooper had been amazing the entire time we were out with Shelly, but the minute I'd mentioned his dad, he had flipped to pissed off. Actually, anytime I mentioned Robert, Cooper would get angry.

"Do you hate your dad?" I finally asked when we pulled into the garage. I shut off the car and turned to him.

He hesitated, obviously thinking about how to answer my question.

"I hate who my father is. I hate the things he's done. Once you know the real him, you'll understand why I am the way I am."

"You're not telling me something, Cooper. I'm not stupid. You know you can trust me," I said softly.

He shook his head. "No, I can't. You're with him, and since you have no plans to leave anytime soon, that puts us on opposite sides. I'm sorry, Claire. I've tried to help you, but you refuse to listen. I've said all I can say."

He climbed out of the car, and I followed. Going inside the house, he didn't stop until we were at the top of the stairs.

"You're not being fair, Cooper!" I said angrily.

"You want to talk about fair?" He laughed. "Every time you look at me, I can see exactly what you want from me. When I try to give it to you, you literally run the other way." He stepped closer to me so that only a few inches separated us. "You run because you're so damn scared of what would happen if you stayed."

I shook my head in denial.

He laughed. "You're unbelievable, Claire. Even now, I can tell you want to run from me before I do something that you *want* me to do."

He stepped closer to me until his body brushed against mine. He reached up and grabbed the back of my head, pulling me to him. His mouth slammed down on mine. I wasn't even surprised this time. I let myself kiss him for a moment, tasting brownies and ice cream on his tongue and savoring the way he felt, before I shoved him away.

"I'm tired of this game we're playing, Cooper. I'm done." I turned and walked away.

I was proud of myself because, for once, I didn't run.

It was too bad that I hadn't looked back. If I had, I might have noticed Robert standing in the doorway to the kitchen. I might have known he'd seen Cooper kiss me. That might have changed everything.

Cooper plagued my dreams again. I knew I was dreaming, but I couldn't bring myself to care. All I wanted and all I craved was Cooper's touch. So, when the feel of someone tugging down my shorts awoke me, I still thought I was dreaming. I smiled to myself as Cooper finished pulling my shorts off and climbed on top of me. I might have even said his name.

When I opened my eyes, I saw that Cooper wasn't in bed with me. All I could do was stare, openmouthed, at Robert. He smiled before lowering his lips to mine and kissing me. He pulled away after a moment.

"Robert?" I asked, still confused, "Am I dreaming?"

He laughed. "No, I'm real. I can promise you that. I made it home a little while ago. All I could think about was how you were sleeping in my bed. I need you, Claire. I need you right now."

His fingers found the hem of my thin tank top and slid underneath. Seconds later, they found my nipples. He pinched roughly, and I moaned, unable to stop myself. My body was still on fire from the dream he'd awoken me from. I didn't even have time to think about the fact that I was lying in bed with Robert only hours after Cooper had kissed me. Instead, I watched as Robert leaned over me and grabbed a condom from his nightstand drawer.

He ripped open the package and rolled on the condom, his eyes never leaving mine. "We still need to get you on birth control."

I only nodded as I watched him position himself over me. I was still wearing my tank top, and he was completely naked as he slammed into me. I gasped at the twinge of pain as he shoved his way inside me. Compared to last time though, this pain was nothing.

My needy body responded automatically to his hard thrusts, and I raised my hips to meet him. He stopped long enough to wrap my legs around his waist before plunging into me again. My nails dug into his shoulders as I felt my body's reaction to him. I'd been so close to the edge already when he woke me up, so I felt myself crash over after only a few seconds. I cried out as an orgasm—my second ever—took control. Normally, I would be embarrassed at the volume of my scream, but I was past the point of caring. My back arched off the bed as I came, and I heard Robert grunt as he found his own release.

After our breathing returned to normal, Robert stood and tossed the condom in the trash. He walked back over to the bed and climbed in next to me. After pulling the covers up around us, he pulled me to him.

"I missed you," he whispered in my ear.

"I missed you, too. I wish you had told me you were coming home. I would've waited up for you."

"I wanted to surprise you." He kissed the top of my head.

"Are you home for good?"

"Yes. Everything is back on track in Pittsburgh. I won't have to leave you again for a while."

I smiled as I relaxed into his shoulder. "Good."

I tried not to think about what had happened since he'd left. It'd only been a few days, but I felt like everything had changed. Cooper had placed doubt in my mind, both with his actions and the photos he'd shown me, and I wasn't sure how to get rid of it. I wanted to trust Robert again, like I had when we first met. Back then, everything had seemed so simple. The only thing I'd worried about was our age difference. Now, it felt like there were a million things between us.

"What did you do while I was away?" Robert asked, pulling me from my thoughts.

I told him how I'd brought Shelly to the house and how glad I was to have her back in my life. He seemed happy that I was able to spend time with her. He even laughed when I told him how much junk food I'd bought for her.

"How was Cooper while I was away?" he asked.

I tried to keep my voice neutral as I replied, "Typical Cooper. He was nice most of the time, but he had his moments of assholeyness."

Robert chuckled. "Assholeyness?"

"Yeah, I made a new word. Don't make fun of me," I teased.

"I wouldn't dream of it. Did he give you any problems?"

I shook my head, glad that Robert could only see the top of it. If he could see my face, I had no doubt that he would know I was lying as I said, "Nothing I couldn't handle."

"I'm glad to hear it. I was thinking about our situation while I was away. I've never given you a chance to get to know Cooper better. I won't lie and tell you that we are your typical father and son, but you're going to be his stepmother soon. I think it's important that the two of you get along. I thought that all three of us could have dinner here at the house tomorrow night."

The thought of Robert and Cooper together made my stomach turn. "That isn't necessary, Robert. I know you two don't get along, and I don't want to force either of you to spend time together when you don't want to."

"Nonsense. I want you to be comfortable with him since he still lives with us. I already talked to Ellie, so she knows to make dinner for all of us tomorrow."

I couldn't help but hope that she would be at dinner as well. With her as a buffer, maybe Cooper would behave himself. I always sensed that he respected her.

"Will she be joining us as well?" I asked.

He shook his head. "No, I want it to be just the three of us."

"Can't wait," I mumbled.

Robert literally cornered Cooper the next morning at breakfast. He blocked the doorway as Cooper was trying to leave. From the pissed off look on Cooper's face, I knew he didn't appreciate it either.

"I want you to be home by five tonight. We're having dinner at five thirty, and I expect you to be here," Robert said as he crossed his arms over his broad chest.

Cooper raised an eyebrow, making his piercing that much more evident. "Who all is invited? I hate to break it to you, but I'm not much for your fancy dinner parties, Dad."

"It's not a party. It's a family dinner. Just you, Claire, and I will be here."

For the first time since I'd walked into the room, Cooper's eyes found mine. I pleaded with my eyes, hoping that he would tell Robert no. I couldn't even begin to describe the fear I felt over having those two in a room together for more than a minute or two.

Whatever Cooper saw in my eyes made him smirk. He turned his attention back to his dad. "Sure thing, Dad. I can't wait to hang out with you and Stepmommy over there."

Robert frowned. "Cut the shit, Cooper. I want you two to get along. If you continue to give her a hard time, I won't think twice about kicking you out on your ass despite what your mother wanted."

Cooper laughed. "Is that what Claire told you? That I've been giving her a hard time?"

"She didn't have to. I know you, Cooper. Claire was nice enough not to say anything though, so don't try to attack her."

"Whatever. Can you move? I have things to do today before I have to come home for dinner," Cooper said, not bothering to hide the annoyance in his tone.

"Five o'clock, Cooper. I'm not messing around." Robert moved to the side.

Cooper was out of the kitchen in a matter of seconds.

Robert turned to me. "What are your plans for today?"

I shrugged. "Nothing at the moment."

"I have to go to the office to take care of something, but I'll be home later this afternoon. If you need anything, call me."

He walked over to where I was leaning against the counter and kissed me. I watched as he turned and disappeared from sight. I couldn't help but feel a total sense of dread over what would happen tonight. My gut instinct told me that whatever happened, it wouldn't be good.

I spent most of my day with Ellie, helping her around the house and then finally helping her with dinner. Robert wanted something simple, she'd told me, so we'd decided on lasagna. I wasn't the greatest cook out there, but under her watchful eye, I did most of it myself. Once it was in the oven, I helped Ellie set the table and clean up the kitchen. She shooed me away after that, telling me to go shower and get dressed.

My stomach churned with nerves as I climbed into the shower. I'd hoped that Cooper would make it home before Robert so that I could talk to him, but I'd had no such luck. I would just have to hope that Cooper would have the common sense to keep his mouth shut.

Robert had promised to be home early, but it was almost five now, and he still wasn't home. I almost hoped that something had come up at work, so he'd have to miss dinner.

I showered quickly and found an outfit for dinner. I decided on a cream-colored button-up shirt with tiny beaded flowers throughout and a pair of dress slacks. I had no idea if my outfit was what Robert had in mind for our dinner, but it would have to do.

I dried my hair and left it down, letting it hang down my back in golden waves. I applied minimal makeup, only putting on foundation, a pale pink gloss to my lips, and eyeliner. Once I was finished, I headed downstairs to wait for Robert and Cooper. Five minutes before five, Cooper came through the door. He stopped short when he saw me sitting on the living room couch.

The heat in his gaze made me swallow. I allowed my eyes to roam over him, unable to stop myself. He looked amazing. His hair looked wild, probably from driving around town with his car windows down. He was wearing a pair of shorts and a black sleeveless shirt that showed off every muscle he had. My eyes finally moved back to his face. He smirked at me, aware of the fact that I'd just been staring at him.

He glanced around the room. "Where's my father?"

I looked down at my hands. "He's not home yet."

He laughed as he walked closer to me. I looked up when he sat down next to me.

"Typical. He demands I come home, but he can't be bothered to show up himself."

"I'm sure he'll be here soon." I looked at the doorway, almost expecting Robert to be standing there. "Cooper, we need to talk. I know you don't like your father, and I know you don't like the fact that I'm with him, but please, *please* don't do anything tonight that will cost me everything."

He frowned at me. "Despite what you think, I'm not out to hurt you, Claire. I'm only trying to protect you." He took my hand in his and gently squeezed it. "I want to tell him to fuck off, but I won't." He glanced down at our hands. "I want you, but it's clear you've made your choice. I won't do anything to hurt you tonight. Our secret is safe."

My body sagged in relief. "Thank you, Cooper. That means a lot."

He nodded. "I heard you last night."

I gave him a confused look. "Heard me?"

"You know, when my father was fucking you," he said, no emotion in his voice at all.

The blood drained from my face. "Oh my God. Cooper…"

"And here I offered to give him some pointers. After that scream you let out last night, it's obvious he doesn't need any. I probably heard you because he didn't bother to close the door. I wonder why."

Robert didn't close the door? I tried to think back to the night before, but I couldn't remember if the door had been closed or not. I'd been asleep when he came in.

"I'm so sorry you had to hear that," I finally said.

He shrugged. "It's no big deal."

We jumped apart when we heard the garage door opening and closing. Seconds later, Robert strode into the room. He seemed surprised to see Cooper and me sitting together, but he said nothing.

Robert shot a warning glare at Cooper before turning his attention to me. "Sorry I'm late. Things at work took more time than I'd thought they would."

I shrugged. "You're here now. That's what matters." I tried to smile, but I couldn't bring myself to do it. Instead, I stole one last glance at Cooper before standing and walking toward the kitchen. "Dinner's ready."

I'd thought I would feel nothing but relief after I talked to Cooper, but I was wrong. Another emotion, one I couldn't quite come to terms with, was plaguing me. I knew what it was, but if I let myself admit that, I'd open my heart to even more hurt.

Sadness—that was what it was. I was sad because Cooper had given up on me so easily. I'd expected him to argue with me, to demand that I forget his father and come to him. Cooper had said over and over that he wanted me. Maybe it was a lie. Maybe all he'd wanted was to get me to want him, so he could leave me hanging, all to prove to himself that he could best his father.

I felt a single tear roll down my cheek. I wiped it away before either of them could see it. I was being ridiculous. Cooper was doing exactly what I'd asked of him. I was with Robert. Cooper…well, Cooper would soon be my stepson. That was all he could be.

I picked up the lasagna and carried it to the table. I placed it in the center before going back to grab the garlic bread Ellie had helped me make. I was surprised to see Cooper grabbing drinks for all of us. I gave him a tentative smile as we passed each other. The softness in his eyes as he smiled back shocked me.

Once everything was on the table, I sat down in my usual seat next to Robert. Cooper and Robert sat across from each other, so that left Cooper on the opposite side of the table by himself.

"Ellie helped me some, but I made most of the dinner by myself," I said too brightly.

Robert smiled as he took a bite. I expected him to praise me even if he might be lying, but he said nothing. I frowned as I took a bite of my own. I was pleasantly surprised when I realized that the food did taste good.

Go me.

"Damn, Claire. This is almost as good as Ellie's cooking," Cooper said as he smiled over at me. He glanced at his father. "Don't you agree?"

"Yes," Robert said as he stared at his son.

No one spoke again as we ate dinner. I caught Robert staring at Cooper, and surprisingly enough, he also glanced at me with a calculating look in his eyes a few times. Cooper didn't seem to notice as he cleared his plate—not once, but twice. Coop really did like it, and I couldn't help but feel a sense of pride over my cooking.

"There are a few reasons I wanted us to have dinner together tonight," Robert said once we'd finished our food.

Cooper raised an eyebrow, but he didn't say anything. I kept my attention on Robert.

"First of all, I want you two to get to know each other better. Cooper, you're not the easiest person to get along with. I expect you to show Claire nothing but respect from this moment on. If you give her any trouble, I won't hesitate to kick you out on your ass."

Cooper rolled his eyes. I wanted to beat my head off the table.

"This isn't a joke, Cooper. Claire isn't going anywhere, so I expect you to treat her as part of this family."

He laughed humorlessly. "The last thing Claire wants is to be treated like the rest of the family. Wouldn't you agree, Dad?"

Robert's face turned red with anger. I looked back and forth between them, confused over what on earth Cooper was trying to say.

"She thinks she knows you. If she had any clue what—" Cooper started, but he was quickly cut off.

"This isn't up for debate, Cooper. Claire and I are going to be married very soon. There's nothing you can do to stop it from happening. I know how you like to tell those lies of yours, but they won't work."

I looked back and forth between them, still confused. "What is going on?"

Robert took a deep breath before looking at me. "Nothing, Claire. Just a debate between Cooper and me. Anyway, I have more news."

"What is it?" I asked, thinking that maybe he had to return to Pittsburgh after all.

"The case I'm working on is going very well. The lawyer I handed it over to when I had to leave for Pittsburgh has done an amazing job with it. I have decided to give him full control over it."

"Isn't that case really important to you?" I asked.

"It is, but you're far more important, sweet Claire." He paused. "Once I handed the case over, I made a few calls. We have an appointment at the courthouse tomorrow at nine."

"An appointment?" I asked, completely confused.

"We're getting married tomorrow, Claire."

My mouth dropped open in shock. "But I thought we were going to wait."

"I did, too. But now that the case isn't in the way, what's the point? I love you, and you love me. We have no reason to wait. I want to make you mine."

I couldn't bring myself to speak. This wasn't supposed to be happening so soon. He'd told me that we would slow down. I couldn't marry him when I was so confused about how I felt for Cooper. It wouldn't be wasn't fair to either of them or me.

Cooper laughed. I turned to look at him. Despite his laughter, there was nothing humorous about him. Every single muscle in his body was tensed as if he was about to spring out of his chair and attack someone.

"Something funny, son?" Robert asked.

Cooper laughed again. "Yeah, there is. Look at her face, Dad. Do you really think she wants to marry you?" He paused. "But that doesn't matter, does it? You couldn't care less about what she wants. All you're worried about is trapping her here, so she can be your little trophy wife."

"You're being arrogant, Cooper," Robert said, his voice tight with tension.

"And you're not? Let me ask you this, Dad—do you love her? I mean, really love her."

"Of course I do! I wouldn't marry her if I didn't."

Cooper grinned. "You're lying. You don't give a damn about her. She's just too perfect to pass up though, isn't she? Young, beautiful, polite—she would be the perfect trophy wife. Plus, she's also naive and trusting, so you know you can bend her however you want. You can train her to be the wife you expect."

"If I didn't know better, I'd think you were trying to stake a claim on her, son," Robert said, his voice deathly quiet. He looked over at me. "Claire, can you give us a moment?"

I looked back and forth between them. They might act nothing alike, but the look of calculated rage on both of their faces made them look more alike now than they ever had.

"Sure," I whispered. I stood and walked away from the table.

Once I was out of the room, I pushed the door closed, but I stopped at the last second and left a tiny opening. I knew listening to them was wrong, but I couldn't bring myself to care. They were talking about *me*, so I had a right to know what was being said.

After a few minutes, Robert spoke again, "Is that what this is about?"

"What are you talking about?" Cooper asked.

His voice was so quiet that I had to lean forward to hear him.

"You want her, too, don't you?" Robert asked.

Cooper chuckled. "Don't be absurd, Father."

There was a pregnant pause before Robert spoke again, "You're avoiding, Cooper. I know the truth, I can see it in your eyes. You're not as contained as you think you are."

I could imagine that Cooper was rolling his eyes.

"What do you want me to say? Claire's a hot piece of ass. I'm sure I'm not the only guy who has looked at her and wanted to fuck her. But if you're implying that I want to steal her from you, don't hold your breath. Everything about her that makes you want her is what makes me want nothing to do with her. She's nice to look at, but I'm not into needy, naive chicks. Have no fear, Father. I'm not trying to steal your newest toy. You can have her."

Cooper's words stung, but I'd needed to hear them. All along, I'd wondered what exactly he wanted from me, and now, I knew. He only wanted to use me for sex and to hurt his father. I closed my eyes, fighting the tears away. I hated how much his confession had hurt me.

Before Robert could reply, I turned and made my way to the stairs, careful not to make a sound. Once I was out of their hearing, I ran up the stairs at full speed and went to Robert's room. Tears poured from my eyes as I dropped down onto the bed.

God, this hurts.

No matter how many times I'd tried to protect myself against Cooper, he'd somehow weaseled his way into my heart. Knowing that he didn't give a damn was the equivalent of someone driving a knife into my chest.

I wiped my eyes once my tears had disappeared. I stood and walked to the bathroom to splash my face with ice-cold water. Robert couldn't know that I'd been crying. He couldn't know how stupid I'd been.

When I returned to our room, it was still empty. I shed my clothes and pulled on a pair of pajamas before climbing into bed and curling up into a ball. It was barely past seven, but I didn't care. This day had worn on me until I was too emotionally drained to continue on.

Just as I was drifting off to sleep, I heard Robert walk into the room and close the door behind him. I ignored him as I willed my body to fall back into slumber. Whatever he had to say could wait until tomorrow.

"Claire, wake up," Robert whispered as he climbed into bed with me.

I ignored him.

"Claire, come on. Wake up."

I groaned as he gently nudged me.

"What?"

"Are you okay? I'm sorry for what Cooper said. He'll do anything, say anything, just to hurt me. Unfortunately, he used my affection for you to do it this time."

I rolled over to face him. "It doesn't matter what Cooper said. As long as you truly love me, that's all I need."

He smiled. "Good. Now that I have you, I can't imagine my life without you. I'm sorry that I arranged everything for tomorrow without talking to you first. If you want, I'll cancel our appointment. We don't have to get married until you're ready."

I stared at him, uncertainty flooding me. As I studied his beautiful face, I forced my doubts away. Robert had been my rock for so long, long before Cooper had come around to mess with my head. I realized that most of my uncertainty with Robert came from seeds of doubt that Cooper had planted in my mind. Yes, Robert could be a bit controlling, but he didn't do it to hurt me. He did it because he cared about me. He loved me.

"No, I don't want to wait," I said quietly. "You're right. There's no reason to wait. I'll gladly be yours."

Robert grinned. "I'm so glad you're saying yes. I thought for sure that you'd tell me you wanted to wait."

"I'm sorry that I made you doubt us. You've done nothing but love me since the moment we met. I'd be stupid to let someone like you slip away."

He leaned forward and pressed his lips to mine. I threw my arms around him as I gave everything I had to our kiss. I ignored the fact that I didn't feel any of the sparks I'd felt when Cooper kissed me. Everything about Cooper had been a lie, from his words to his actions, but this was real. Robert was real.

Robert groaned into my mouth as he pulled me tighter against him. Before I knew it, our clothes had disappeared.

Robert had left early this morning. He'd stumbled out the door, mumbling something about keeping tradition, as he had put his hand over his eyes. Apparently, it was bad luck for the bride and groom to see each other on their wedding day.

As soon as he'd left, Ellie came barreling through the door. I yelped in shock since I was still naked, but she only laughed as she walked to the closet.

"Go shower," she called from the closet.

I kept the sheet around me as I grabbed some clothes out of the dresser, and I hurried to the bathroom. After a quick shower, I returned to my room to see a white sundress lying on the bed. A pair of white sandals sat on the floor in front of the bed.

"Let's make you beautiful." Ellie smiled at me.

She dragged me back to the bathroom and forced me to stand still as she curled my hair. Then, she pulled part of it back into an intricate twist that I knew I'd never be able to do. She finished it off with enough hairspray to choke me.

Once my hair was finished, she moved on to my makeup. I closed my eyes as she ran liner under and over my eyes. Eye shadow and mascara followed. Once that was done, she applied foundation and blush. With a light pink lipstick, my lips were next.

She refused to let me look in the mirror until I was dressed. She dug through my underwear drawer and found a pair of light-blue panties. I laughed at her choice of something blue. I took off what I was wearing and pulled them on. Next, I pulled on the dress and then my white sandals.

"There. Done," I said excitedly.

"Not quite." She took something out of her pocket. It was a necklace made of pearls. "You have something blue, your shoes will be something new, and this is your something borrowed."

"Thank you, Ellie," I said.

She clasped the necklace and let it drop around my neck. "You look beautiful. Go look at yourself."

I walked to the full-length mirror and gasped in shock as I stared at myself. I looked good, thanks to Ellie. The woman looking back at me didn't look anything like me. She was sophisticated and gorgeous. Her hair and makeup were perfect. The dress fit in a way that flattered her.

"Wow," was all I could manage to get out.

"I told you that you looked beautiful. I need to run home to change, but I'll be back in just a few minutes. Then, I'll drive you to the courthouse," Ellie said as she squeezed my arm.

I pulled her into a hug, shocking both of us. Ellie was the closest thing to a mother that I'd ever had.

"Thank you…for everything," I said as I released her.

"You're welcome, honey. I'll be right back." She slipped out of my room and closed the door behind her.

I stood in front of the mirror for a few more minutes before finally looking away. I took a deep breath to calm myself as I looked at the clock. It was almost eight. In an hour, I'd be saying my vows to Robert. I would become his wife. The thought terrified and excited me at the same time.

Once I realized that my heart wasn't going to stop hammering away in my chest, I gave up on trying to be calm. I took another deep breath before opening my bedroom door and stepping out. I walked down the hallway and then down the stairs. Once I was in the living room, I sat on the couch and stared at the far wall.

I was so lost in my own head that I didn't notice when Cooper stepped into the room. In fact, I didn't notice him at all until he stopped in front of me, blocking my view of the wall. My eyes widened in shock as I looked up at him.

"Claire…" he said, his voice hushed.

I tried to smile, but after hearing his words the night before, I couldn't bring myself to do it.

"Cooper."

He sighed. "Claire, I—"

"Don't." I held up a hand. "I don't want to fight with you today, Coop. It's my wedding day, and I refuse to let anyone ruin it for me."

His nostrils flared in anger. "Ruin it? No, we wouldn't want that. It looks like you found your happily ever after, didn't you? Lucky girl."

"Yes, it looks like I did." I defiantly stared up at him.

"At least for now. Soon enough, I'm sure you'll realize the error of your ways."

It was my turn to be angry. "Just stop. I refuse to listen to anything else you have to say. Since the day I met you, all you've done is confuse and hurt me. You don't give a damn about me, do you? The only reason you were nice to me was because you wanted me to trust you, and it almost worked, Cooper. You should be proud of yourself for fooling this stupid, naive little girl."

"You think I'm the one trying to fool you? Seriously? You're more of a fool than I thought. Everything I did, everything I told you, was to help you. You have no idea who my father is!"

I laughed. "Really? And I know who you are?"

"I've never lied to you, Claire. Never."

"Bull!" I shouted. "Everything you told me was a lie. The way you touched me was a lie, too. You only wanted to hurt your father, and you tried to use me to do it."

I yelped when he yanked me up by my arm. It didn't hurt, but it was still shocking to be sitting one minute and standing inches away from Cooper the next.

"I tried to protect you, but you refused to listen to me. I do care about you, Claire, or I never would have tried to intervene." He paused, trying to compose himself. "And when I touched you? That wasn't a lie either. I've never wanted a woman the way I want you. You're beautiful inside and out, and I want you to be mine."

I stared up at him in shock.

"There are things you don't know about my father, things that would terrify you. All I wanted was to get you away from him. He *will* destroy you, Claire. He'll break you until nothing is left."

"You're lying," I said, but my voice held none of the anger from before.

Why is he doing this to me? How can he put doubt into my mind every time I look at him?

"Am I?" He raised an eyebrow. "I'm not a good man, and I've never claimed to be, but next to him, I'm a fucking saint."

"Let me go, Cooper. Ellie will be here any minute," I finally said.

He shook his head. "I've let you go enough times."

He jerked me against him and kissed me like he was starving. I gasped in shock as I tried to push away from him. He held me tighter as his tongue surged into my mouth, igniting fire inside me. I finally stopped fighting and wrapped my arms around his neck. He groaned as his hands roamed over my body, finally stopping on my ass. He squeezed my ass, causing me to moan into his mouth. The kiss seemed to go on forever before he finally pulled away.

"Tell me *that's* a lie, Claire. Tell me that you feel nothing when I kiss you."

I looked away from him, shame covering me like a cloud.

"That's what I thought. Leave with me right now. I'll protect you, Claire. I swear, I will. Just please don't marry him."

"Ellie will be here any moment," I finally said as I untangled myself from him. I sidestepped to escape him, and I headed for the door. My mind was a mess.

"So, that's it?" he called out from behind me.

I stopped and turned to look at him again. It took everything in me not to run into his arms even though I did think he was crazy. No matter how much I disliked him for hurting me, the magnetism I felt toward Cooper would always be there.

"That's it." I continued on toward the door.

"My father had my mother killed."

His words chilled me to the bone.

I stopped dead and turned back to him. "What did you say?"

"You heard me, Claire. I've spent the last year living with a man I hated because I have to. I have watched his every move, waiting for him to slip up. My mother was going to leave him, and he found out about it. She knew far too much about the things he's done to get where he is today for him to let her go, so he had her killed."

"And where's your proof?" I asked, barely breathing. This was *it*—the thing he'd been trying to hide from me all this time.

He looked away. "I have nothing concrete. All I know is that two days before she died, he withdrew fifty thousand dollars from one of his accounts. A month after her death, I received a letter from a lawyer in Virginia. He was going to represent my mother in the divorce. It was smart of her to contact someone from out of state since my dad has every lawyer in the area in his pocket. She gave the lawyer a letter to give to me in case anything ever happened to her. She said that if something happened to her, she wanted me to know why. She told me to get as far away from my father as I could because he'd hurt me, too, if he got the chance. But I couldn't. I can't just walk away when he's still out there, living his life, while my mother is in the ground. That's why I still have my private investigator on his tail. My father is bound to slip up at some point, and when he does, I'll have all the proof I need."

I stared at him, openmouthed. "You're lying."

"I wish I were. Do you really think I'd be here if I didn't have to be? I hated him before, Claire, but after I found out the truth, I felt such a burning rage inside me that I wanted to literally kill him. It took everything in me to keep from taking his life. My father isn't a good man. I've tried to tell you that over and over, but you've refused to listen. Now, you're in as deep as I am in all of this. He won't hesitate to hurt you, too, if you step out of line."

My heart raced as I tried to process what he had told me. He thought Robert was a killer. *This is insane. Cooper is insane.*

"Besides a letter and a bank withdrawal, you have no proof that Robert did anything wrong," I mumbled. "You can't really expect me to believe this."

Cooper glared at me. "I wouldn't lie about something like this, Claire!"

"Yes, you would! You've tried to come at me from all angles, hoping to tear my relationship with Robert apart. And now this? You've lost your mind, Cooper. Your hate for your father has literally driven you insane!"

He stalked across the room, and I shrank back, suddenly terrified of him. I had absolutely no idea what he was capable of at this point. I remembered my first assessment of him. With his tattoos, piercing, and nasty attitude, he screamed bad boy. Now, with him suddenly only a foot away from me, that thought came back tenfold. No, he wasn't a bad boy. He was dangerous and insane.

"I'm trying to protect you, Claire. Goddamn it!" He ran his hands through his hair.

I'd never seen him like this. Cooper was always calm and in control, but now, he looked crazy.

"I don't need your protection. Stay away from me," I said as I crept backward. I reached behind me and found the doorknob.

"You know what? I don't even fucking care anymore. Go and marry him, but don't you dare expect me to help you when you see the monster lurking just under the surface. I'm tired of trying to save someone who can't be helped."

"I would *never* ask for your help," I spit out.

He grinned, but it was cold and almost lifeless. "Run along then. Be Robert's little whore."

For the second time in my life, I slapped someone. It was ironic that it was the same person as before.

He jerked back, shocked at what I'd just done. I took the opportunity to throw open the door. I ran outside, not daring to look back. I saw Ellie's car parked in the driveway, and I nearly cried in relief as I ran to it.

She gave me a bewildered look as I all but jumped into her car.

"Claire, what's wrong?" she asked.

I shook my head. "Nothing. Just drive."

I looked back one final time. Cooper was standing in the doorway, staring at the car. I fought tears as we drove away.

I closed my eyes and tried to calm myself as I felt the car driving toward the courthouse, to my wedding, and away from Cooper and his crazy thoughts. I couldn't help but wonder if I was running from a hurricane and straight into the path of a tornado.

God help me, how did my life come to this?

Deception, Book Two

Coming Early 2015

TAMED TEASER
COMING NOVEMBER 4, 2014

Prologue

I hated the word *whore*. It sounded so…filthy. I'd been called a hundred different names before—slut, skank, ho, bitch, just to name a few—but when someone called me a whore, it would set my blood on fire.

As I stared down at my fate, I realized that they'd all been right. I was a whore.

There was no coming back from this.

I closed my eyes and willed myself not to cry. I'd done this to myself. This was what I deserved.

I hadn't always been this way. Once, a really long time ago, I'd been innocent. I'd worn my heart on my sleeve. I'd looked at every day like it was a gift instead of the plague that it really was.

Life was so damn hard. I hated it. I'd hated it for years. More than once, I'd wished that I hadn't had to deal with it, that I hadn't had to deal with *him*. But fate had laughed at me, repeatedly throwing him in my face just when I thought I'd healed.

How could I tell him this when he seemed to hate me more and more every time we saw each other? How could I tell him this after what she'd done? I was no better than her.

What was once innocent love and attraction had morphed into something…volatile and ugly. By now, it was almost unrecognizable.

Who am I kidding?

It had never been innocent. We'd seemed to be incapable of innocence, especially him.

I would never survive this. The moment I'd seen him, even though I hadn't wanted to admit it, I'd known that I would never survive *him*.

Tears fell down my cheeks, but I brushed them away as I stood and walked out of the room. When I reached my bedroom, I picked up my cell phone and dialed the only person I knew I could trust, the only person who knew every secret of mine—my best friend.

"Hey, Amber. What's up?"

"Chloe, I need you," I whispered.

Chapter One

Four Years Earlier—May

Charleston, West Virginia

I ran a brush through my dark brown hair and looked in the rearview mirror, making sure that my makeup was still flawless. Bright green eyes stared back at me, outlined perfectly with black eyeliner. My tanned skin was practically glowing from happiness. I smiled to myself as I adjusted my low-cut tank top so that it revealed even more of my cleavage. I climbed from my car and tugged on my shorts, inching them up my legs bit by bit.

I'd fought with myself for almost an hour as I debated on what to wear to surprise Chad, my boyfriend for the past year. Today felt special for some reason. I wasn't sure why, but it did, and I wanted to look perfect.

Along with my two best friends, Logan and Chloe, Chad and I had graduated from high school just last week. We only had two months to spend together before we would head off for West Virginia University in the fall. He'd be there with me, but I knew things wouldn't be the same, so I wanted to make sure that this would be a summer he'd remember.

I'd grown up alongside Chad in Charleston, West Virginia. We'd been in classes together since kindergarten, but it wasn't until last year when I'd really noticed him. I wasn't the only one who had taken notice either. He'd come back to school a good two inches taller and heavier with several pounds of all muscle. Girls who had barely looked at him before had started hanging around him, flirting their hearts out, but he hadn't paid them any attention. Instead, his eyes had watched me.

Two weeks after school had started, we had officially become an item. Since then, we'd been inseparable. He'd even earned bonus points by winning over Chloe and Logan.

I was a lucky girl, and I knew it.

I grabbed a grocery bag out of the backseat and locked my car before walking up the sidewalk to his parents' two-story brick home. I grinned as I slipped my key into the lock and quietly opened the door. After closing it behind me, I put my bag down by in the entryway and crept up the stairs to Chad's room.

His parents were on vacation this week, and instead of going with them, he'd decided to stay home and spend some quality time with me. Unfortunately, he had called early this morning to let me know that he had to cancel our plans because he'd ended up with food poisoning.

Instead of letting him wallow in misery alone, I'd decided to surprise him and nurse him back to health with some soup, and I would do it all while looking fabulous, of course.

When I reached his room, I grabbed the doorknob and slowly opened the door. I didn't want to wake him if he was sleeping.

The smile left my face when I saw his bed. He definitely wasn't asleep. My world crashed around me as I watched him fucking Carrie Jenkins, head cheerleader and complete whore. I stood there, frozen in shock, while he let out a groan as he came. He kissed her forehead before pulling out and standing, his back still facing me.

He slipped on a pair of basketball shorts. "As usual, that was great, babe."

Carrie mumbled something before burrowing underneath his covers. When he turned around, facing my direction, he had a satisfied smirk on his face, but it died instantly when he saw me standing in the doorway.

"Amber!"

I shook my head as he took a step closer.

"Don't come any closer, or I'll rip your dick off."

"It's not what it looks like," Chad said, his voice pleading.

I laughed. "It's not?"

"It's exactly what it looks like," Carrie said from the bed.

I looked over to see her sitting up and stretching her arms above her head, putting her breasts on full display.

I rolled my eyes. "At least one of you is honest." I turned to leave.

"Amber, wait. Please," Chad said.

I ignored him. I hurried through the hallway and down the stairs to the front door. He caught up to me just as I was getting ready to open the front door.

"Amber, please."

I jerked my arm out of his grasp and leveled him with a death glare. "We're finished, Chad."

"I know I messed up, but it won't happen again."

"How many times?" I asked quietly.

"What?"

"How many times have you slept with her?"

"This was the first time, I swear. She's been coming on to me for months, and I finally caved. It was the stupidest thing I've ever done. You mean the world to me, Amber."

I laughed. "You're lying through your fucking teeth, Chad. I heard what you told her. The sex was great—*as usual.* This wasn't the first time you've slept with her, and I doubt that it will be the last. Enjoy each other. I can't think of two people who deserve each other more."

His mouth hung open, obviously shocked that I'd caught him in another lie. I stared at him, truly seeing him for the lying asshole that he was.

"I can't believe I thought I loved you." I laughed bitterly. "Never again will I give you the power to hurt me. Stay away from me, Chad, or you'll regret it."

I turned and threw open the door, and then my eyes landed on the bag I'd put down earlier. "By the way, I brought you some soup and crackers to help your stomach."

I picked up the bag and tossed it at his head. It missed and crashed into the wall, knocking several pictures onto the floor. I watched as the glass in the frames shattered, but I didn't even care.

I turned and walked out of his house. I promised myself that I would never look back, but I'd always remember this day. It had changed everything for me. I wasn't naive and innocent anymore. Chad had stolen that from me, and I'd never forgive him.

Maybe I should've thanked him. He'd shown me what the world was really like.

He was the beginning of the end for me.

***

I walked into my parents' house, wiping my tears away.

"Oh my God! What happened to you?" Chloe shrieked.

I looked up at my best friend. How many times had I comforted her while she cried over her abusive mother? It was more than I could count. We'd been best friends for years, but I couldn't think of a time when I'd cried in front of her. I was sure it had been a shock to see me walking through the door, sobbing, with my makeup destroyed.

"Chad," I whispered, sitting down on a barstool in the kitchen.

I rested my elbows on the counter and willed myself to stop crying. He wasn't worth all this pain. He wasn't worth anything.

"What did he do?" Chloe pulled out a stool and sat down next to me.

She reached out and pulled me to her. I cried into her shoulder for a few minutes before pulling away. I winced when I saw the black stain, courtesy of my eye makeup, on her white shirt.

She looked down and frowned when she saw what I was looking at. "I don't care about my damn shirt, Amber. Now, tell me what happened."

I stared at her, almost smiling at the fierce look on her face. It seemed foreign on her delicate face. Despite the way she'd been raised, Chloe was fragile. I always told her that she reminded me of a porcelain doll. She thought it was because of her blonde hair, blue eyes, tiny frame, and creamy pale skin. It wasn't the reason, but I let her believe it. No, it was because she was so damn breakable. I was always the strong one, the one who defended her and offered to crack skulls whenever she needed it.

I wondered how I'd fair with a porcelain doll coming to my rescue. We might both end up broken by the end of this conversation.

"He cheated on me. I caught him screwing Carrie Jenkins about half an hour ago."

Her eyes widened in shock. "Chad? You can't be serious. He's so…nice."

I nodded. "I wouldn't have believed it if I hadn't seen it with my own eyes. He called me this morning to tell me that he was sick, so he couldn't meet up for our plans. I thought I'd surprise him and help him get better, but I was the one who got the surprise."

Chloe shook her head. "I'm so sorry, Amber. I really thought he was a good guy."

"It's not your fault. I didn't see it, and neither did Logan."

She gave me a small smile. "We could always call Logan. I bet he could kick Chad's ass. Logan is bigger, and he'd probably even enjoy doing it for you."

I shook my head. "There's no point. Logan would end up in trouble. And for what? A lying, cheating asshole who doesn't deserve even a second of our attention."

"You're right," Chloe said finally. "Are you going to be okay? I've never…it's just…you never cry."

Her voice was so soft and gentle that it nearly brought me to tears again.

"I'm not okay right now, but I will be. I'll survive."

She pulled me into another hug. "I'm right here. I'll make sure everything gets better for you." She took out her cell phone, one that my parents had paid for, and started texting.

"What are you doing?" I asked.

"Texting Logan," she said as if it were the most obvious thing in the world.

Truthfully, it was. The three of us were inseparable. We would be best friends forever—or at least until Chloe realized that Logan was in love with her. Then, I wasn't sure where our terrible threesome would end up.

"He'll be here in a few." She stood and walked to the fridge.

I watched as she opened the freezer and pulled out a tub of ice cream.

She grabbed three spoons out of a drawer and turned to face me. "Come on, I know just what you need."

"What?" I asked wearily.

"An ice cream party while we watch the hottest man alive slay evil things."

I smiled. "*Buffy* marathon?"

She nodded. "*Buffy* marathon."

When Logan arrived twenty minutes later, we'd already put a huge dent in the ice cream. He took one look at the television and sighed before dropping down on the couch beside me.

I handed him a spoon. "We're going to spend the day getting fat. You might as well join us."

He smiled before glancing over at Chloe. His eyes were still on her when he took the spoon from my hand.

Finally, he looked back at me. "You good?"

Chloe had obviously told Logan what was going on.

"I'll survive. Now, shut up, and let me watch Angel. I think he takes his shirt off in this one."

He rolled his baby-blue eyes. "Oh, goody, I can't wait."

I laughed as I elbowed him in the stomach. He'd obviously been working out more. My elbow felt like it had collided with solid steel.

Asshole.

Logan was one of the prettiest guys I'd ever seen but not in a feminine way. No, no one could describe him as feminine, that was for sure. His sandy blond hair was cut shorter than normal for summer, but he pulled it off well. His eyes were a bright blue, and his lips were full but not overly so.

I'd watched him for the past four years. His once round baby face had gradually sharpened into the strong face of a man. Once upon a time, I'd thought that I cared about Logan as more than just a friend.

I'd even tried to act on those feelings, but he'd kindly told me no. I'd been hurt until he explained how in love he was with Chloe. Once he'd admitted his feelings, I wasn't sure how I'd been so blind to them. From then on, I'd notice him watching her daily with a desperate look in his eyes.

Even though he'd shot me down, I never held it against him. He'd been sincere with his regret. That had been much easier to handle than watching my boyfriend of almost a year fuck someone else.

Tears welled up in my eyes again, and I silently cursed myself. I tried to hide them, but Logan missed nothing. He wrapped his arm around my shoulders and pulled me tight against him.

"This show isn't all bad. At least Buffy is hot," he said without taking his eyes off the TV.

God, I love this boy. Leave it to him to let me deal with my tears without drawing more attention to myself.

I glanced over at Chloe. I only wished she could love him the way he wanted her to. Out of all of us, Logan deserved happiness the most.

ACKNOWLEDGMENTS

For me, this is the hardest part of my books to write. I need to thank so many people, and I know I'm going to miss a few of you!

First, I want to thank my husband. He's stuck with me since the beginning. If it wasn't for him, I would never finish a book. His support means more to me than he knows. I love you.

To my son—You make me smile when I have absolutely nothing to smile about. Your giggles, silly games, and sarcasm (I wonder where you get that from!) make every single day brighter.

To my author friends—I love you all so much. Without your constant support, I'd be a raging lunatic by now. I love tossing ideas back and forth with you ladies. You rock my socks. A special thanks to Tijan for being my rock. I swear, I'd marry you if you lived closer. Please never stop answering my 3 a.m. Facebook messages. If you do, I'll hop on a plane and hunt you down.

To my blogger friends—GAH! You guys are so incredible. Seriously. Several of you have been with me since the beginning, and I don't know what I'd do without you. Your dedication to everything *book* constantly amazes me. Nicole, Kristy, Amanda, and Amber—please never stop Snapchatting me.

To my parents—I love you guys. That about sums it up. You're always there for me, no matter what.

To my readers—Thank you. Just, thank you. You're incredible.

Made in the USA
Charleston, SC
25 November 2014